Monkey See

by

Pete Grohoski

ISBN: 978-0-6151-6847-0

This book is for my sons. Not as much as to read but as it is to show them that anything can be done when a person puts their mind to it. Regardless if the book is great or absolutely horrid I will still be proud. I can still say I wrote a book because I wanted to and didn't quit. Even if the only copy out there sits on my coffee table.

Love you guys!!!

"The dictionary is the only place where success comes before work."
Mark Twain

In the small town of Pikerville, evil has taken up residence. In a matter of a couple of months the town that was known to be peaceful has come to the brink of hysteria .Within the next two months the town will witness and host an evil that not many towns have fathomed or even heard of. The damage that will occur when there from the murders will be irreversible. Evil has no sympathy and it does not discriminate. Age, race, religion is irrelevant. If you breathe you are then a possible statistic and if you are lucky your death will be swift and God will save you. The town of Pikerville is about to change. Evil has moved in and no one is safe.

Sitting down and reading a newspaper or watching television can make a person fall into a comfortable trap. The belief that all the violence, or negative acts cannot happen to them. We feel we are in a bubble where these occurrences do not happen. Like the little domes with water and when you shake it, it snows. There is no room for violence here, we don't allow it. This is a world that cannot be affected by a shake. A bad day at the office, late on the bills, nothing serious that can destroy a person's life. If that shake however becomes more violent where a crack or a hole where our little bubble is violated, then everything changes. Those activities have now become real in our world where we now take notice and can't ignore them.

We can only get a feel of some of the badness in the world if we were there. Somethings can't come to us like certain natural disasters but murder, that can come to us and we may even let it in without knowing.

Those articles we read, the news breaks we watch have us feel sympathy for those victims. Instead of sympathy how many feel that relief that they were never those articles. The next time we walk into a store and look someone in the eyes we maybe looking into the eyes of a murderer. It is said there are 500 serial murderers in the United States right now. There is a chance at some point in our lives we have crossed paths or engaged in conversations with these people. Now consider that and see if the next time you are in public alone you don't look over your shoulder for that someone that could be a murderer.

Where am I? Everything is black. No lights. No sounds. What is happening? I can't move my hands or legs. They are tied. I am sitting in a chair.

How did I get here?

I can't see a damn thing. Something rubbing up against my face. Shit! It's must be a mask or a bag. My head is contained. Too much shit to comprehend .I feel light headed almost like I am delirious.

I can smell like a musky scent but it is not that not strong. There is a cold chill on my skin but it is October. Maybe I am in a basement.

I am alive, right? God, what is going on? Ok think   I went to work, had lunch, and was done .I was entering my car at about 7pm then....I...I... I can't remember. Damn it, think. What the hell is going on? I must be kidnapped.

Ok wait a minute .Kidnapped? No can't be. Right? What for? Money? No way, I am far from rich.

"Help me!! Somebody Please!!!" Shhh. Nothing I must be alone. Somebody save me. Maybe a gang kidnapped me? Robber? NO too much effort taken for a few bucks. Has to be something else. I can't think of anyone that would do this to me.

I have...NO wait! Maybe this is someone that I just laid off at the firm. Yes, yes that is it. It has to be.

I laid off 32 people at the firm. It was not expected by them and I had to decide which of them to lay off. Instead of upper management taking a percent cut for the next year or two and saving some jobs they decided to lay off the employees. They kept their salaries. There was no notice just swift extraction of the people and forced to leave in 1 hr. Clean their desk and out of there.

"I can get you your job back!! I swear to God, I will!" .They hear me? Nothing. No sounds. Why me? I know I laid them off but I was told to. I am only the head of Human Resources but they know I get the commands and I follow them. No think Matt, think. Wait. That television interview channel 6 .I was interviewed about the layoffs later that day. Damn it, I said "I did what I felt what was right for the company. Some people have to realize not everyday is a happy day. They may have to actually work a little harder in finding a new job." I am sure it did not help that the reporter pointed out I was one of the people who voted against my salary being cut. Shit what an asshole I am.

As he sits there strapped to the chair, he starts going through all the possible people who may have it out for him.

Ok, ok now just who could it be? Only 32 possible people .I have that guy in the mailroom who just got married. No he is way too small to have moved me and taken me down. At 245, 6 foot I find it hard to believe he could have done this after all he is 5 foot 7 and 170lbs. No maybe it was Mike Nosam. Yes he is freaking big enough and... CRACK!!!!

"Hello? Who is there?" Someone is close .I think in a room next to me .I see no lights but this damn mask or whatever could be screwing my vision up. "Listen if this is about your job I will hire you back. I will forget about all of this." Something is being moved. I still can't tell how far away but it is not in this room. Ouch! My neck hurts as I turn it around. I must have been hit from behind and knocked out.

I think that sounds like a door opening. Is that a click? Looks like a light through the bag. It is a thick cloth so I can't make out images in the room .Huh, I see a silhouette of I think a man.

"Please don't hurt me. I can make it up to you. Is it money? I give you what you want. I have plenty saved." I have a few thousand saved from living alone and being efficient. Saving for when I meet that right woman and decide to tie down. Now I have saved that money to save my life .Funny all that saving and I may not even live to see my dreams. Maybe I am being punished and this is a sign. Well you have my attention God .Please let me live, I promise to stop mistreating people if you let me get out of this alive.

I hear him moving around the room. He is to my left and sounds pretty close. He can do whatever he wants to me and I will not even see it coming. What would he do to me? Shoot me? Stab me? What if he does something inane like slicing me up? No. I don't want to die slow .God if he is going to kill me make it swift.

Thoughts of death pass through bounded man's head and he is terrified. His body is trembling to where the chair is now thumping on the floor. His pants now have become warm and wet from urinating himself.

"What are you gonna do to me?" He is moving something like dragging a table across the floor. "Answer me damn it!!I have a right to know what I am here for!!" Why does he not answer me? Shit he is touching me. He is taking off this hood. It is dark in here. I can see just shapes.

He is behind me I felt his hands but they were very soft like leather gloves were on him.

I think something across the room is moving.

What the fuck is he doing? He is taking off the bag. Now I can see who this is! It is dark and I think I am in like a basement or something similar.

 He is pulling my head back from behind. He has a watch on it looks like 855pm. What is he doing? He is shoving something in my mouth a sock or something. I can't speak only yelp. Wait his gloves are not leather! They are rubber.

God what is going to happen?

He has a scent of strong cologne like it was just put on. He is strong for I can't move my head. He is tilting my head back and now shoving something else in my mouth .A hose, I think. No I think it is a funnel with a 3-4 inch hose attachment at the end I think. It is dark but I am certain of the object. What is he doing with it? .WHAT?!?!?

God it is so hard to breathe. I feel lightheaded I hope I don't pass out or maybe it is best. My throat is drying up this cloth is taking everything out of my mouth and swallowing has become painful.

The funnel is cutting the inside of my mouth. God it hurts. It is partially down my throat to where I want to gag.

I am not very religious but I pray to you God to forgive me for my ignorance to you. Never acknowledging you till now. I know I am going to die and hope I die quick. Please hear my screams, my prayers Lord.

He is holding a container over my head and tilting it towards the funnel.

I see a liquid coming out as if in slow motion. I am going to literally drown .My life is flashing before me and my death is now coming to me as if in a movie, frame by frame. I hear it hit the funnel and start that swishing sound of going down.

I now feel something hit my throat. It feels cold, NO wait hot!!! Real fucking hot! It is burning my throat!!

What the hell is it? I try to make noise but I can't .I am choking.

JESUS! Is this fuckin acid!??! That is why the rubber gloves!!! My God my throat is getting eaten away. My chest is feeling hot too. It is running out of my throat like there are holes. It has made to burn my chest and stomach. I can't breathe I am blacking out.

I can no longer feel the pain I must be almost dead. The nerves traveling from my head to my body are being eaten away. I can no longer feel anything.

I look forward to my death.... it is here..... I hope you burn in hell you bastard......

MMMMPPHHHH!!! Help me!! Let me go!! What is going on? Wait.

A woman strapped to a chair fights violently to release herself from the restraints placed on her. She too is masked .She runs through visions of what horror that are in place for her.

What is that noise? Sounds muffled .I hear movement or a struggle. I hear a voice like someone trying to talk but their mouth is covered like mine. Seems like another voice too. Not talking though maybe there are 2 people in here .No wait that other sound that is not a sound of pain but that of laughter. A series of chuckles. The kidnapper, what else can I call him, is torturing the other person. I can hear cries of help in the muffled sound. It is a high pitch sound that is terrifying me. What is happening to him? The chuckles seem to be replaced with another sound, a laboring grunt. The kidnapper is doing something, something that requires force. He is laboring .The sounds from both seem to be climaxing they are peaking. I wish I can see, I am so scared .The sound of a human squealing like a pig is terrifying and not being able to see why is absolutely ungodly.

Wait the sounds they....they stopped. The squealing, the chuckles, everything is stopped. It is so quiet. An eerie calm comes upon the room. What is next?

What is that? Sounds like something being broken .Like wood snapping or something plastic. It stopped.

Oh my God! Maybe someone was just killed. What was he doing to him? I could hear him gasping for air and then someone laughing quietly. Almost like the killer was quietly proud of what he was doing. I couldn't do a damn thing. I am completely helpless, I can't scream with this damn tape on my mouth.

Am I next? Shit! I can only hear what is going on. Tape and blindfold is on so damn tight I think I have cuts and am bleeding. That warm feeling on the right side of my face has to be blood. Could have been when this psycho broke in and attacked me. The hit to my head and throwing me down into the basement could have broken me open. I must have blacked out at this point and he put this bag or mask on me. I can't break through this tape on my hands and feet. Hog tied or at least I think. My hands grow numb and so do my senses. I am tired from fighting to get. I can't even beg for mercy or answers.

What does he want? He asked for nothing just beats me and ties me up. Can't be money, he hasn't asked or maybe he just wants my valuables. I have none here. I am not rich or important Jesus I am Deja Williams. A nobody. He hasn't raped or touched me outside of wanting to hurt me. I am confused and so scared. Will I still be alive in five minutes? I can't stop shaking from crying.

Who is this other person I think he just killed? My neighbor? Am I still in my house? I can't tell. It is damp and somewhat cold but I can't tell. Just too much going on. Why no dialogue? Just like me his interaction is silent.

This can't be personal otherwise I would be alone. He must have brought this guy with him or maybe someone saw him come in. He was just checking up to see if everything was ok and he was trapped when he came inside. Jesus, what is happening? Why me?

What was that? He just touched the side of my head. Right? Am I crazy? He did do that. My God he is getting ready to hurt me or even kill me. I can feel he is near me lurking like an eagle watching the river for its dinner. My chest feels tight and getting tighter. It is fear. The fear is like an anvil on my chest restricting my air. It is tough enough trying to breathe with the tape and mask but now I feel light headed. I feel like I may pass out but the fear keeps me from doing so.

Ouch! I am being picked up by my hair with the mask on! I am being moved .He is picking me up. Ughh! I am being thrown in a chair or something close. What is he doing? He stopped .It is so quiet, so dark, so scary. Shhhh Deja get yourself together stop crying and sobbing. I can't hear what is going on.

Where did he go?

Wha? My mask is being removed. Ouch, he is ripping it off. My hair is stuck with it along with the blood and sweat that gathered in it. I can't open my eyes, the light is so bright .I need a second to adjust. I want to see who this person is. Ok now I can see something the shapes are being sharper and more focused .I am in my basement on the old kitchen chair I put down here when I purchased my new kitchen set last month.

I have been down here for an hour or so. It is 915.

Oh MY GOD!!! There is a body. A man's body lying across the basement about 20 feet away. He is lying behind the basement couch. I can only see him from the chest up. What is that in his mouth? It looks like a … Shit! What just touched my face? It is him! He is behind me pulling my hair back behind my ears. His hands are soft and smooth. I try screaming but everything is mute. Maybe I can see what he looks like .Ugh, I can't turn around .His fist or forearm just hit me on the left side of my face. He is now straightening my face out with a hand on each side of my head. His hands are black. He is going to break my neck. No he stopped. What is he thinking?

He is behind me again with it looks like a silver slender metal object. A stake? Spike? I can feel him pull my hair straight and it looks like that metal object has a hole in it like a sewing needle. Ouch he is yanking my head back. I can't see what he is doing in the mirror. Damn it; move so I can see what the fuck you are doing. There I can see he clamped the end of my hair in that hole. Thank God my hair is almost down to my ass otherwise he would have to rip it out to stretch to the spike.

Ow! He is holding my forehead with his left hand, now almost giving me a headlock across the top. GOD!!! What is he doing? He is putting that spike in the back of my neck God. WHAT IS HE DOING? My God he is driving through my neck. He is trying to KILL me!!! Stop. Stop!!! I can feel my muscles being torn through. I can hear the muscles tearing inside my head like a newspaper. I can't move he has me trapped. Jesus what is going on?? Let me be dreaming!!

Please let me die now!!I can't handle this pain. My neck is so warm from the blood escaping. Ugh, shit the spike has popped through the back of my throat. I can feel it touch my tongue in the rear of my metal I can taste blood and metal. I am urinating myself. I can't control anything right now!! You sick fuck I hope you burn in hell!!

I am having trouble breathing, I am choking the spike is now moving across the top of my tongue toward my lips. Blood and the spike have closed my passageway almost completely. I can feel it behind my front teeth. It is pushing through them breaking a few. I can feel them breaking apart. What have I done to deserve this? I wanted to have a family and grow old with them. It is over I am weak and can't feel my body.

I can see he set this up in front of the mirror so I can watch me die. , OH God, the spike is coming through the tape across my mouth. It is bloody. Bastard took the bag off my head so I can watch his sick, twisted display of torture. I am dying, can't think or stay conscious. This is not the way anyone should die .I had so much to do and so much to say. I love …you mom a..a.nd ….da……….

A 1999 Dodge Ram races down a busy street in a tiny town of Pikerville, in Pennsylvania outside of the city of Philadelphia. Doing rolling stops and not pausing for the yellow lights Mason Kade figures to be at the crime scene in 10 minutes. Mason who is 3 yrs detective is a smart young detective. Deciding two years after high school to become a detective after holding signs for traffic work he made a decision .Being careful not to spill his hot chocolate while going around the corner, he nervously taps the wheel. Knowing he is heading to a double homicide makes it the fourth murder in a month and a half. The town of 33,000 is at unease with just the two which no suspects or clues are available. Reward has been discussed because of the cases becoming stymied. Not much more has been done due to the optimism that something will break.

He wishes that this double homicide is a murder suicide which will prevent a ground swell in the public. The possibility of it getting out to the big city news or even national media if this is a fourth murder would be devastating. It could possibly encourage the murderer to do more. Or it could have him leave the area which would leave them unsolved which leaves the town in fear .A murder has not happened for twenty years here everyone is green to how to solve and deal with it. The previous two murders have stumped the detectives, forensics and others involved in the case. No clues, hints, fingerprint not even a simple fiber. The emptiness of clues has Mason questioning his peers. Are they not qualified? Can't be but to have no murders to have some work with does not help. This is not Philly or New York where murders are an average of once a day.

He has thought about bringing a profiler in. Now this maybe the next step if these murders are similar. The murders were both done in a vacant warehouse outside the town. Both tied to a chair, hands and feet. The only differences are in the way they were murdered. One was choked with a towel from behind where it was turned and twisted form behind till where it was so tight it snapped the guy's neck. The second was where cargo straps were wrapped around the torso and tightened across the chest by the clamps that tie down the cargo on trailers till where the ribs were snapped. He died from internal bleeding and suffocation.

The victims have really nothing in common. One was an auditor for the IRS and the other was a parking ticket officer.

One was black the other was white. Eliminates racism.

The auditor was 28 and the officer was 46. No common friends or enemies. Both had their wallets still on them untouched. So many questions and the answers are few and far between. How did they get there? How were they caught? Why were they caught? Robbery? No. Ransom? No. Then what?

He turns onto the street of the double murder. It is about six blocks out of town so the houses are about fifteen feet apart, a quiet older neighborhood overall. He pulls up in front of the house where a crowd gathers. The forensics are there waiting. Mason gets out of his car and approaches the two story Cape Cod house. It is 1025.

"Hey Mace" says the officer standing at the base of the steps leading up to the house.

"Hey, how did we find out?"

"Neighbor saw the door open and called the cops when no one answered her when she called into the house"

"Same as the others?"asks Mason.

"I haven't been in but word is that it is bad, real bad. Couple of guys came out vomiting or needing air. "

"Ok thanks." Hmnn sounds nothing like the others .Sort of good if that could be possible. He enters through the front door and brushes past a pair of officers whom he overhears saying how this was like watching those serial murder films at the FBI. He passes through the living to the kitchen wear the stairway to the basement is. He notices everything seems in its place. Nothing is broken and a clean environment. He sees pictures of possibly the victim and a group of her friends. Mason jogs down the steps to the basement where about a dozen cops and forensic people are.

"Hey Mason. How is it?" says John Milker an older detective dressed up in an expensive suit. "Good till now. You're all dressed up, hot date?" "

"Nah a wedding and then I heard this over the radio and well you know.."

"Yes I know" .Meaning yes I am thinking and praying not another 2 victims.

"Where are the bodies John?"

"Mason listen I have been doing this for 16 years and I have never seen something like what you will see. Take a deep breath and be ready. It is disturbing. "He points Mason to another room where three cops are standing in the doorway pale and almost frightened looking.

"Is it him again?"

After a brief pause." I am not sure."

Mason walks into the room and sees a male in a chair. Blood is all over his chest. Taped to a chair by hands and feet. By his feet is a puddle of a blood and some rocks or small stones. Mason feels squeamish as he approaches the body looking at the ground. He bends over to take a better look at the pebbles, stops dead in his tracks and notices those are not pebbles but teeth.

Slowly elevating his eyes from the floor upwards past the man's torso he looks at the head. His mouth is torn open and the throat looks ripped out or torn open. A site that makes Mason fell extremely ill never saw this isn't any courses he thinks to himself. Doesn't help there is a sick foul smell coming from the body.

"What is that smell? He is freshly killed so what stinks to all hell?" asks Mason to a CSI agent.

"We believe a chemical of some type is involved over here but tests need to be done. So don't touch anything without wearing some protection."

"Gotcha ya. Good point."

"So what do you think?" asks John.

"I am not sure" He looks around for hand prints or footprints from the killer but has seen nothing. "Has anyone found anything?"

"No but come here you are not done" John is standing by the woman's body. Mason approaches and sees the body but is unsure what he sees.

"What the fu..? My God."

"Yep we have a sick fuck here." John walks away shaking his head not daring to do more then a glimpse at the body. Mason on the other hand looks almost trancelike at the body.

What is happening here? He sees the woman's body bloody from the mouth down. He knows the blood came from the mouth. Coming out of her mouth is her hair .It was pulled through the hole made in the back of her neck and hangs out 6 inches or so. He sees the spike that was used lying next to her.

I have to get out of here he thinks to himself.

"Anything found to help us out?" "Nope. Looks like a possible struggle in the stairway but everything is otherwise fine. We know she lives here, Him on the other hand we assume is a boyfriend or a neighbor who was in the wrong place at the wrong time. Both murdered down here. No one heard or saw anything .With their mouths gagged that explains a lot."

"What is the chance this is him?"asks Mason hesitantly.

"Honestly Mace we are not sure what to think. This is not like the first two murders .They were clean or impassionate. These have blood, rage and hatred all over them .Maybe this is real personal A love triangle possibly if it is not him."

"Four murders in over a month by more then one person? No this has to be the same guy .Maybe it was a love triangle, he was part of it and snapped. Hell, he has killed two already so what is he afraid of? Another life sentence?"

"Well Mace hopefully when the guys are done here they will have some clues to help us. I will go around again and see if anyone can help out .I can meet you at the station then, ok?"

"Ok, I need to get out of here .I feel lightheaded. I need to clear my head .It is bad enough the last two murders are a mystery this only confuses things more"

"See you in a little Mace?"

"Not tonight I will be in tomorrow early." Mason walks back up the steps towards the front door .He pauses and walks into the dining room. He looks around for pictures to help identify the guy. The woman is single and with no children. The house is neatly taken care of but no sign of any male companionship in the house. So who is this guy in the basement? He heads in the kitchen where there are too many bodies and he is sure he will not find anything they haven't already looked for. He doesn't want to look anymore .He knows he will not find anything. The frustration of no clues and unfamiliar with a murderer or serial murderer doesn't help either. He goes outside down the steps towards his car not noticing the scores of cops and investigators looking for clues. He does look about twenty feet away where a crowd has set up and it is bigger then the last murders crowds. Mason looks at their faces .Some wondering what is going on while look like they are in fear they saw a ghost. He can hear a murmur of people wondering what is going on. A couple of people are trying to get his attention. Mason looks away and pretends he is looking for something so he doesn't need to scare them more by not being able to answer their questions to the way the want. He heads towards his vehicle.

The smell of death has left his lungs but it remains in his mind. He knows it will be a long night ahead.

Lance Grohan decides to head to the local Giant for some Orange Gojo and air freshener for his house. Just an hour and a half ago he was taking someone's life now he's singing and tapping his hand to the song on the radio in his vehicle. Feeling like he just finished a big project at work on time he has a sense of accomplishment. Reflecting on the night's efforts he rethinks if he made any mistakes. From the moment of the abduction, through the killing, and the cleaning up he ponders if he was careless at all. After thinking it through he lets out a grin. Not uncommon for a man as meticulous as himself to think like this. A job well done he thinks.

What could I have done to make that son a bitch suffers more he thinks. He starts thinking of ways he could have punished him differently. Almost depressed he comes up with another form of death. To him it is not about the killing it is about how you torture them to where they beg for death .Slow deaths are what he desires, if it is quick then he feels unfulfilled. His reasons for killing are the same and the punishments are also it is the route he takes to get there.

It is 1022 pm and the roads are pretty clear not much traffic at this time of night. He is on route 724 and approaching route 100 and about to head north. He gets on the route and starts to accelerate .He starts to drift off again into his thoughts. He approaches a red light but it is not the light that catches his attention but the red and blue lights off to the side of the road before the light. His starts to feel his heart beat pick up, his breathes start to become shorter. A roadblock .Could they already have found the body? How? Did someone see me? He remains calm but the questions start to multiply in his head.

He looks to see if he can pull off and back up but the road has no shoulder to pull off into. I can get through this. There is no evidence in here, no more then the other vehicles around me. The traffic is a light backup there is a sign not too far away but he can not make out what is says. He turns down the radio and starts thinking how to act if they ask him out of his vehicle but wait he starts to chuckle. He can read the sign "Sobriety check point ahead" it says. He starts laughing out loud.

Whew that was a scare he says to himself. Ok this shouldn't take to long. He is three cars deep and they seem to only be asking every third or fourth car. He starts to approach the pylon cone where an officer is off to his left and three off to the right. There are three more off to the left further down testing some people for drunkenness. He starts to put his window down on his 2004 Explorer.

"How are you doing officer?" The office does a quick visual on his 2004 black Acura

"Not bad sir. How is your night? Where are you heading?" Says the tall average build man. Seems like a nice guy Lance thinks. The officer starts to bend down and lean towards the vehicle.

"Pretty good here .I am just heading up to the Giant to get a few things for the house."

"Oh the wife sent you out?" he laughs.

"No not here .Just a girlfriend but we live apart".

"Had anything to drink tonight? " He makes a sniffing sound with the motion "What is that smell? Smells not like alcohol but maybe like a cleaner or something ". Oh God think fast Lance thinks.

"Oh that smell just stripper from stripping wax floors. Don't worry any alcohol here."

"Sure?"

"I can take the breathalyzer if you want. I have nothing to hide"

The officer almost ponders what to do next but then comes up with a decision.

"Well I bet you had a long day and the worst thing is probably a few too many vapors for you. Listen, get on and have a good night."

"Oh officer it has been a great night". Lance starts to pull away from the cone. Wow that was unexpected .Never thought about the scent to others .Pretty quick thinking, he thinks to himself proud of the cleverness. Deep down inside he enjoys the challenges that are unexpected and his cunningness to get by them. He approaches the light and proceeds through it.

"I guess I stink he was trying to tell me" he laughs as he pulls his vehicle into the lot

Within a minute he pulls up to the Giant and gets out of his vehicle.

What scent am I into tonight? He looks at the air fresheners and grabs the mulberry .Nah, he puts it down and grabs for the vanilla. Something a little passive is suitable tonight. Not in the mood for something strong, need something to relax me-to set the tone for bed. Next what better then a big bowl of ice cream to end a good day he feels. He heads to the frozen food aisle and gets an Edy's M&M chocolate ice cream half gallon.

He starts to head towards the dairy aisle but stops. Hell this isn't my grocery trip I don't want to be out all night I have to work tomorrow. I'll just get the rest of the stuff on Sunday.

He heads towards the checkout first for the self check out but notices Amy is out register 6 with no customers. He heads towards her.

"Hey stranger" he says.

"Hey Lance how are you? What brings you out this late at night?" she replies.

Amy is 21 years old with a one year old boy. The father left her when she found out she was pregnant. A piece of white trash is what he is thought of by Lance. She is a good girl with tough circumstances that he feels for. Admiring her will to succeed with being a single mother who refuses welfare because she believes she is better then that and will prevail. He started becoming friendly with her when he moved in the area 3 years ago and started shopping there. It was when he saw her reading a book outside about pregnancy and what to expect when he struck conversation with her .It was there he started to learn about her .From there he made it a point to talk to her or keep in touch with her about her pregnancy. He had become friends with her and even visited her in the hospital when the baby was born.

He never had thought of her as some side piece he could work on but as a friend. He is 13 years her elder and never believed in relationships with such younger halves. Feeling that was inappropriate for any reason. Yet he didn't want to stop talking to her for he enjoyed her views on life at her age. How refreshing he thought when they talked. A woman who has grown up at mind regardless if it was forced by pregnancy or intentional.

He remembers the time he saw her at the store putting a couple of containers of baby formula back on the shelf .He approached said hi and asked why she was putting them away. Money was the reason. Her boy was a month old. She was staying at home for 6 weeks to bring him up till her mom would quit her job and watch the boy through the day while she worked. She saved up money for the situation but with a loser father to not help out the money was going quick because the boy was a big eater she said. Feeling the urge to help her he bought her groceries that day for her and added 3 containers of formula. Never mentioning it afterwards for a guilt trip or a way to get her to sleep with him. He every now and then asks if everything is ok financially to see if he needs to help but she has had things go her way in the last year getting a full time job at a local doctor's office, setting appointments which has great pay and benefits, plus the part time job at the store 3 days a week for a few hours.

"Well I need to satisfy my ice cream fix. Also needed a couple of little things. How are you and little man? Still a little sumo wrestler?"

"We are great. Yes he is still my lil sumo guy. That boy just loves to eat."

"Well that is good to hear. So why are you working tonight? You don't work nights." He looks around and sees no one approaching and figures he can chat with her for a few minutes and not get her in trouble.

"Well someone called out then they called me and asked me to come in for 3 hours. My mom was over and said she would take Forrest home with her till I was done."

"That is nice of her .You are still at your day job right? Curious why you are picking up more hours."

"Yes it is great I just thought that with Christmas coming around in a couple of months it would not hurt to pick up a couple of hours here and there if it didn't affect Forrest."

"Wow someday you will meet the right guy and make him a great wife. Your boyfriend was obviously immature and dumb. Your maturity and ambition must have scared him off. Maybe you needed to have no job or future for him to like you."

"Yep I can't believe I was with that loser .What was I thinking?" They laugh together.

"So is that manager treating you right?" he refers to a manager who a couple of months back was treating her like an ingrate because she was a single mother and looked down upon her. He must have thought she was irresponsible and would treat her unruly by monitoring her breaks down to the second. Amy took Lance's advice and chewed him out. Since then he has backed off and treated her no different then the others.

"Yes not a word or dirty look. He realized I am not one of these moms looking for handouts from people. He actually shows interest in my life .If it is genuine or not is another thing."

"Well if he or anyone ever gives you any problems or issues let me know. I'll take care of him" He gives out a light laugh. You will never have to worry about that he thinks to himself.

"I will, I know you will be there for me. You are a good guy Lance."

."Thanks".

She finishes loading the bag. "It is $13.29." He hands her the check card and she processes it. He signs the receipt and grabs his bags.

"Well you take care of you and your family. I am sure I will see you real soon."

"You, too ,Lance. It was nice to see you. Bye"

"Bye." He walks towards the exit and out towards his car. A happiness comes upon him causing him to smile. As he reflects on the night's activities he says to himself "Tonight was a good night." He rid the world of a pompous ass and then converses with the type of person, whom is the reason he does these things.

He gets in his vehicle, pulls away and heads home. He thinks how is girlfriend is so similar to Amy. Maybe that is why he likes Amy too. She has the qualities and attitude he likes in a person. The same qualities his girlfriend, Jill has. He picks up his cell phone to call Jill. He wants to say hi to her before he goes to bed. She works as a nurse at the local hospital and she should be on her break right in about 5 minutes. He turns onto his street and makes a left into his drive way. He pulls up gets out and makes his way into the house.

He lives in a small Cape Cod like house. Kept nicely mainly by him but his girlfriend does pick up after him on his lazy days. He turns on the lights empties his bags and puts the stuff away. He heads into the bathroom and takes a shower. He scrubs hard to get the smell off his skin. He gets out and dries off quickly. He is anxious to have a bowl of his favorite ice cream and talk to his girlfriend before bed.

He reaches in the drawer for a spoon and into the cabinet for a bowl. Being a fickle person he never leaves stuff out on the kitchen counter or in the sink. If he uses something he immediately cleans it and puts it away. He scoops out his ice cream and goes to the living room with his little buddy, his bulldog, Traegen, following him. He has had his dog for a year and loves him. He spoils the dog as if it was his child. He came with the name Traegen, meaning "warrior" in Latin, because the dog has no quit in playing or whatever he has his mind. The ice cream does not last long and he spends about 15 minutes watching CNN to see if anything interesting is happening in the world today. He is tired and decides it is a night.

He heads into the kitchen cleans his things and lets the dog out. A few minutes go by and Traegen, the dog, does not come back to the deck. He heads out the door and calls for the dog. "Traegen! Let's go boy. He looks out into the darkness hoping to see the shadow of the dog approaching. "Traegen, where are you?" Tapping the cell phone against his leg impatiently he starts to open his mouth "Tra.. There you are boy" Dog comes out of the shadows of his yard. "I swear there must be a female dog out there and that ties you up. Oh well, at least you are getting lucky tonight." He laughs as he pets the dog behind his ear. "Inside." The dog goes in, with him following. He locks the door turns out the lights and heads upstairs to the bedroom with the dog. He jumps into bed and calls Jill.

"Hello" a female voice says.

"Hey babe."

"Hey what a nice surprise .What did I do to deserve this?"

"Nothing" he says" I just miss you "

"Awww I love you. You are so sweet. So how was your night? "she asks.

"It was great. Remember Amy at…." He continues his conversation with her for about ten minutes. She has to cut the conversation short due to a high amount of emergencies coming in this night. He says good night and hangs up with her. He stares at the ceiling and lets his mind take over.

Fifteen minutes later Lance starts falling fast asleep with the sound of a fire horn in the background.

Mason grabs his scanner and turns it off. He doesn't want to hear what or where the fire horn is all about. He has been home for 40 minutes and is now lying in bed after eating a late dinner at Burger King. His girlfriend is in the shower and has to get to bed soon for work tomorrow. Mason stares at the ceiling and dwells on what his next steps are. Does he have a serial killer? Why are these murders so different? The rage or hatred that was involved bothers him. The fact of two murders at the same time does not help either.

He tries to get his mind off of the night and try to give Melissa some time so he can hear about her day. He feels guilty that the last few weeks they have not had the time they normally have spending together. With the weekend coming up this was their escape to be what they use to be –cohesive couple. God that feels like years ago he thinks to himself when they or he had no issues when work was over. He misses her incredible smile that attracted him to her. Being the same height as him he always said they always see eye to eye.

He laughs to himself. She has long brown hair, big brown eyes and somewhat resembles Ashley Judd. She goes to the gym frequently for circuit training and is in great shape. He started to redo his diet when he started going out with her. He is a thick big boned guy but very strong. He is solid and wanted to tighten things up for her. They use to go to the gym together regardless of the time but now with the murders things have changed.

The water turns off in the master bath and a few minutes later Melissa walks in. Just wearing a t shirt and white thong she lays next to him. She says nothing but runs her fingers through his hair. Knowing Mason is really bothered by the situation she says nothing but hopes he initiates the conversation and hopes she can comfort him.

"Hun I am worried. I know I said I would leave work at work but…"

"Mace this is bigger then your normal day at the office .I want to help you if I can. Even if I have no clue what to say I can listen if that helps".

"I know. You are so good to me but I can't get this out of my head and have a feeling it is going to keep going. There are signs that I hope I am misreading. I have a feeling these murders are related. I have not dealt with even one and now I have four to deal with. I have no experience and am unsure what the next step is if forensics come up with nothing tonight."

"Well did they tell you they found nothing?"

"No I haven't called nor will I. I will wait till tomorrow when I go there .I need sleep otherwise I would get none knowing the answer either way."

The tone is of uncertainty in his voice. She can hear it and knows Mason is very uneasy. He is the happy go lucky guy who surprises people with his knowledge and smarts. He tends to throw people off by being the funny guy but don't mistaken that for he is a man who absorbs everything that he is around or taught like the desert sucks in a rain that comes in rarely. He always spoke of when he became a cop he hopes he never gets bored .He hopes for some chases and some action but this is way above and beyond anything he wished for. From when she met him 3 years ago at the gym she has never seen him so preoccupied. Always worried about everything else other then work this is a new area she has not really dealt with him. Even with his college work he always seemed to be with her in mind and body when they were together regardless of exams or what have you. This has made her realize how serious of an issue it is .It is not just a death by accident or even a murder in a domestic dispute but something that has no rhyme or reason.

"Maybe something will go your way. If it is a serial murderer I am sure he will screw up .Nobody is perfect."

"I sure hope he is not but you're right if there is nothing after four murders then I will be concerned. A person who makes no mistakes will keep going till he makes one and if it is tiny he will be even more meticulous." He looks towards her. "Remember how I hoped for a little action this is not what I meant. This is way bigger then just a murder. I can feel it. "

She wants to ask him what happened but she decides to can catch it in the paper or ask him tomorrow after work after the shock subsides. It maybe time to change the topic and then go to sleep.

"You will do fine babe just wait and see what happens tomorrow, k?"

"Yeah you're right."

"Still wanna catch a movie this weekend?" she asks anxiously.

"Of course as long as I am not busy."

She knows if he is then the killer struck again.

"Good night. I love you." He turns towards her and kisses her on the lips. A preoccupied kiss but for this night she is very satisfied.

"I love you too."

He pulls her into him and squeezes her hard .She knows he needs support and she holds his arm tight to her breasts. She knew being the girlfriend of a cop had its dangers but this is different. The town looks to him and the other officer's .They expect protection and answers. Right now he can offer neither. She usually tries to keep everything quiet and get her information from other sources so she does not frustrate Mason with the questions. She doesn't want to tell him her opinions but she feels there is a serial murderer and this will get uglier. Being in a small town where the police force is not quaint to murders this is a perfect scenario for a murderer.

He is restless but remains close to her. Maybe this weekend she can try to restore some of his sanity .Maybe.

It is 8am and Lance jumps up in bed.

"What the ..?" he says startled.

"Aww did I scare my little baby?" It is Jill just coming in from work. Enjoying the scare she gives him she straddles him and leans back.

"Shouldn't someone be getting ready for work?"

"Nooooo" he says playfully. "Remember I worked extra hours the last few days in return for today off? Oh I am sorry honey I should have paid attention to you when you talk." he kids. He reaches up and grabs her down towards him. Her blonde hair dangles is his face causing him to blow it away so he can see her green eyes. She is a cute, feisty and playful woman. Someone whom Lance always cared for since he met her at a job 5 years ago.

He brings her lips down to his and starts to kiss her lightly. Running his hands down her back to her ass he grips it and gives it a light spanking.

"Ow", she says smiling.

"Have you been a bad girl?"

"Very ", she says smiling evilly.

"Well we know what happens to bad girls don't we?"

"Hmnn . No tell me"

He starts kissing her deeply while he starts to unbutton her shirt. He pulls back her shirt and reveals her breasts.

"My what do we have here?"

He flips her over to her back and starts kissing her down the side of neck.

"You smell great and look even better".

"Thank you" she says quietly as she pulls him closer. The moans of pleasure start to pick up and eventually get louder and muffle out the sound of the news on the TV in the living room where there is an update about the 2 murders from the previous night.

The police station is a like a circus in the middle of summer .People all over some not knowing what they are doing while others are trying to get away from those to save their sanity. In this case it is the cops not knowing what is going on .The media from the region is starting to gather with the possibility of a serial murder in the town.

Mason arrives to work with a deep sigh of depression knowing his day will be long with no relief.

He parks around the back to avoid the media around front who are doing everything to get an interview from any police officer who is within ear shot.

Mason gets out of the car grabs his lunch and scurries in. He heads to his office puts his lunch in his personal fridge and proceeds to the conference room where a meeting with all officers and detectives is being held at 830. He enters the room and sees Ron Silk, the captain there.

"Hey cap. Any good news? "

"Hey Mason we will discuss that in a couple of minutes." His body language is fidgety and Mason knows the answer just from that.

"In other words nothing. Well how far has the news spread?"

"Just Philly news nothing national but give it time."

"We need to get some clues, Cap. If we don't it will only get uglier. Even if we need to give a reward so be it. The public wants something from us to hang their hopes on. "

"I agree and guess what someone has to go out there and answer something otherwise they will be more suspicious. We don't need false info out there where it can possibly hurt us", the captain states.

"Well it is not like we can drop any clues on anyone" Mason says with a sarcastic and frustrated tone.

"I know it is a serial murderer. No possible fucking way, these are not related."

"I agree Mason. Let's head into the room."

They enter the meeting room where it is a full house of cops and detectives numbering thirty plus men. There is a hum but not of excitement .It is of uncertainty .Men scared to ask one question .The question that everyone knows the answer but everyone hopes is wrong.

Ron heads to the podium in the front of the room where he starts to speak.

"Thank you for coming. I know this is a room of questions. Questions Like 'Is it a serial killer?' or 'Do we have any clues? ''. Well as of right now I have no answers for either of them. Forensics is dedicating every resource to figure out something to get this investigation started. We have nothing .No prints, hair, fibers, DNA, spit, nothing –absolutely nothing"

The room's temperament turns negative .Bodies that were erect are now slouching and faces are now scouring everywhere but the front either to think of solutions or to avoid the truth or hearing this may lead to another murder or murders.

"I want everyone's ears open out there .I don't care what you do ask pimps, hookers, druggies, bums your neighbors, hell put your damn ears to the ground if that is what it takes to get answers but do something."

An officer in the back raises his hand.

"Go head John"

"Ron, all we are hearing is negative info can you tell us what you do know about the murderer? Like a profile what he maybe like. Any thoughts of what you think we are up against? Four murders and you are telling me there is nothing?"

Taking in a deep breath the captain tries his hardest to answer the question but realizes his skepticism is very noticeable and can't bring down the morale.

"I am not a profiler and a possible list of what the killer may do, or be interested in is being worked on. What I think? It may mean nothing but since you asked this is what I came up with. The killer is unorthodox he seems to kill either in a demonic induced episode or he kills with a precision of a surgeon from beginning to end keeping everything clean and in some sense professional. We are not sure why his murders are different but we are trying to see if there are any relations between the victims where maybe he hated some more then others. Maybe he like some of his victims and killed them quickly with no torture while others prayed to God for a quick death..."

"Is there a time frame when we think the next victim is found?" asks a heavy set officer in the back.

"As far as we know it could be now as we speak that is why we need to go and attack the streets. This has been two months since the first murder and we have nothing. The feds may come in if they see we are in the dark."

"Is that so bad if they do?" asks Sallie Pone, a ten year vet. Mason looks over at her and can see the woman who is strong and confident sounds cracky. Before Ron can respond Mason answers the question.

"No it is not bad but being one of the lead detectives we don't want to show the public we went outside the department to deal with this. They want security and we must give it to them."

"Is it security or pride Mason?" she rebuts back but as he opens his mouth she realizes he is taken back by the comment and did not deliver the question the way she wanted. Mason looks at her face and then realizes she just didn't deliver it the way she wanted .He avoids a confrontation and lets her continue.

"I mean it has been ten months and today Cap says we have nothing. I mean seriously I can't be out there and reassure people when I myself question us. Not us as a group but are we prepared physically and mentally for this? Our forensics compared to the Feds is no comparison. Maybe we have nothing but maybe their equipment gets us something ours couldn't. Do you see what I mean? The public won't see it like what you say. Maybe after it is over but not till we come up with something."

Mason looks around the room and sees the force looks like she has taken a weight off their chest. A question that was finally posed but everyone too scared to ask. A force that realizes maybe it is out of its league. He pauses and succumbs to the idea-somewhat.

"You are right maybe our manpower doesn't have what it takes but not because we are not intellectually capable but because our equipment and experience with mass murderers doesn't allow us to rise and show our knowledge. I will look into getting some help with the captain but I will tell you I believe in every one of you out there regardless how long on the force. I would pick the same group even with the most sophisticated equipment given to me. We will prevail .If you have questions from the public or even yourselves call me, come to my office and I will help out anyway I can. For now ..."

A knock on the door and the desk clerk pops his head in." Hey cap, media wants to ask some questions and they are not going anywhere. Any answers?"

Ron looks over at Mason. Then back to the clerk."Yeah right now. Give me a minute; I will be out front then".

Mason finishes "Well let's get out there and be alert look at everything twice someone somewhere knows something and they may not even know it. Anything else cap. Sorry for interrupting."

"No you did better then I. You are the lead guy and probably you should conduct these meetings with the force updating them"

"No problem."

"Ok guys get out there. Good luck."

As the room empties Mason approaches Ron.

"You think we are losing them? The force seems disoriented, not sure what to do next."

"Yes Mason I can see this is starting to affect their judgment amongst other things."

"I can't have a force out there being negative or lethargic to where the public panics and decides to have a mob mentality because they have given up on the police force and decide to take the law into their own hands."

"Yes could be real bad especially if we come up with a suspect or a person of interest. That person would be convicted the moment something like this would happen. A lynch mob. Would be a hunt like for Frankenstien back in the 40's movies."

"I agree." The captain's face says it all. He has a sign of fear and worry.

"I need you to be strong and try in every meeting to keep these guys optimistic Mason. If you have to stretch the truth for them to become upbeat so be it. Try not to focus on the negative shit, hell that is all they will be dealing with for the next God knows how damn long."

"Understand captain. In a way maybe the Feds aren't such a bad idea. The public may feel more comfortable or give them a piece of mind if that would happen. Their equipment is more advanced and the extra manpower would be a help."

"Yes it would but you understand some will lose faith in us if that happens also? God forbid another would happen they would be crying to bring in the feds to resolve it quicker and guaranteed."

"True but how about first we try solving it ourselves and second let's not think about future murders considering we haven't through the first four." Mason pauses and reruns the last couple of sentences through his head.

"God damn, you hear me? First four murders? Remember when we just had our first? It just seems to double every time not giving us a chance to tackle the first and here we are working on the third and fourth!" With that shakes his looks outside the window and can't believe what he is saying. Ron comes towards and pats him on the back

" Mason listen don't let this break you down. You are under a lot of stress and this weekend go and get away. Go with your wife somewhere and escape for a couple of days. Clear your head. If the guys see you are frustrated and about to break what do you think that will do to the force?"

Mason turns around and looks at him. "I know .Can't have them see me like this. I gotcha cap."

"I understand Mason hell I can't be negative to anyone either but my better half and I know when something bugs me it bugs her to so I watch what I say at home. At the same time when I am down or frustrated you need to go to your other half for strength, there is nothing wrong in that."

"I know cap I have done with mine too. Actually we are going out to the movies this weekend to try to get back to normal."

"There you go .You know what you are doing .You should have cut me off instead of wasting my hot air on you." Ron then gives a light hearted laugh to break the tension. Mason catches and chuckles back with a smile. He then looks out into the hallway and notices and the faces looking at them and realizes the media is waiting. They both realize they have to end their conversation and Ron heads to the door and Mason stops him.

"What are you going to say?"

"Exactly what I know .Nothing." The only difference they will think I know something and am hiding it. Of course if I do it right."

"Ok. I am going to the coroner and see if the autopsy found anything." Mason heads out the room and towards the exit out the rear towards his car. In the background he can hear the murmur of the media approaching Ron.

Lance lies next to Jill. "Damn honey were you in the mood?" He laughs at the comment he made.

"Maybe ", she smiles.

"Well I am gonna get going to the store and run some errands. I know you are tired get some sleep and I will be back. Maybe we will go out for dinner tonight .K, hun?"

"No problem. Let Traegen out too for me? Then just lock the doors .There were two murders last night and I am feeling a little scared probably because I am tired."

"Two?" he asked inquizitely.

"Yeah just lock the door?"

"Of course, love you."

He gets his sweat pants and t shirt on then heads for the kitchen. He walks past the table and looks at the newspaper Jill brought in.

He starts to read the headline as he looks towards the television and sees the Ron Silk answering questions for the media.

"How many murders were there last night captain?"

Lance listens closely to the press conference almost intrigued by what is going on.

"Two."

"Are they related to the previous murders? Asks a reporter.

"It is too early to say and we don't want to cause a panic in case we are wrong."

"Are there any similarities captain?"

"Again it is too early to say. All I can tell you is we have two dead people and we are waiting for some evidence to be processed and when we do we will update you."

"Do you have any suspects or witnesses?"

"Right now, no."

"Were both murders related?"

"We are not sure but they both happened in the same scene."

Lance chuckles saying under his breath "Very clever Cap but you can do better then that."

He proceeds towards the television and turns it off. He has heard enough and shows no interest in the news –for he already knows it. These guys know nothing he thinks to himself and that is the way it is going to stay. He calls for the dog,"Traegen, Come boy! Let's go out!!" With that the stocky brindle bulldog comes galloping into the kitchen and scurries past Lance to the outside where the yard is fenced in. Lance watches the dog run out and chase a squirrel. He then closes the door. He goes to the counter finishes off his drink.

He grabs his keys and heads towards the car.

Mason arrives at the coroner's office.

"Hey Jen. Doc in?"

"Yes he is. He was expecting you would be in early." states the receptionist in the town's small coroner's office.

28

"Oh he was?"

"Yes. He was a little antsy, you know unnerved."

"Hmph .Maybe he has something good to tell me. How is your family?"

"Oh good my mom hit the church raffle last week."

"She did? What was the prize?

"Believe it or not a 50 inch big screen TV." She says with a hearty laugh.

"There you go maybe you can get it from her if you act like a good girl."

"No chance .She will not give up Jeopardy on a big screen for me. Hell I will probably get the Philco out of the kitchen and she will put the on in the living room in the kitchen."

Mason laughs and passes her desk."Well tell her congratulations and you take care till I see you again."

"No problem but I have a feeling that won't be to far down the road. Unfortunately."

"Unfortunately I agree. See ya."

Mason heads down the hall to a door which takes him to the basement where the coroner William Janes is .He walks through the hallways which are green cinder blocks. How appropriate is it to have a coroner's office in an old psychiatric hospital which is small a housed 15 of the state's mentally disturbed people? These people were housed here because doctors, back then, would examine them. Sounds normal but rumors were spreading back in the early 1900's that this place was for the insane but tests were being performed on them. Tests from trying new medicines for their problems to just testing new drugs that were irrelevant to their problems. They were just rumors but then a patient escaped and killed three people. He ate his victims .When he was captured a tube in the back of his was sticking out like a feeding tube but much too big. There were also scars and bruises looking from electrical shock. When he was interrogated he was not much help .His tongued was cut out. When the police noticed all of this they searched the hospital and found supposedly other atrocities. This had the hospital shut down and the patients were sent elsewhere. The documents that were written about the hospital were later stolen and to this day the stories of the hospital and treated as an urban legend.

With the story in his mind Mason always gets an eerie feeling .I am sure there are some scary stories here after dark the doc has.

He walks through the door and finds William there.

"Hey Mace, How are you?"

"Do you need to ask? Tell me you found something out that will help me out."

"Well this guy is very smart. Everything he does not only leaves you no clues but there is nothing here I can work with .No special type of knife or a bullet. Just stuff you can get anywhere. Or something that someone found in their attic and decided to use it from 50 years ago that have no tracking anymore."

"Well aren't you the bearer of good news."

"Sorry Mace but I haven't stopped trying. Anything you can tell me?"

"No not really. I feel certain this is the work of a serial murderer. Surprise surprise."

"I had that feeling too. Unless there is something in the water then everyone is just killing someone .Do you know what you are dealing with?" the coroner asks meekishly.

"Bill we are blind .the murders have like nothing in common besides they are all dead."

"Have the Feds called?"

"Nope not yet but if it happens again I am sure we will be getting a call."

"I was thinking 'God these people have nothing in common with each other.' Their deaths are so strange .What is the thinking?"

"I think he justs likes torture. A sick fuck. God knows what he has next in mind."

"Or who?" interjects Bill.

Yeah well back to these people. Anything? Self defense marks? Fibers? anything?" Mason asks with the hope of something good to come out of Bill's mouth.

"No marks. No trace of fibers or skin under the fingernails. Now the lady with the rod driven through her mouth had her teeth broken out .Honestly this is one sick bastard. The rust on it tells me the spike was either left outside or it is very old. Regardless I see nothing coming off of it that will help us. I think it is a spike that is used for pitching big tents. You may want forensics to take a deep look at it. The straps on the other guy broke his ribs from being tighten only question I come out of this with him is was he still conscious as they snapped."

"Great." Mason sighs and heads to the door slowly.

"How about tox reports? Anything in their blood? "Mason asks sounding almost desperate.

"Well the early reports show nothing abnormal. No drugging that I see. When the other tests come in maybe something will pop up then but if history repeats itself like in the other two murders then we will come up empty."

"I'll call you if anything comes up but don't sit by the phone."

"Trust me I won't".

"Hey Mason?" Bill asks with a tone in voice that is different from the conversation.

"What's up?" Mason pauses near the door and turns around.

"Keep your head up. You know you will catch him."

"I am sure. Just the question is when."

"It was bound to happen. We have been lucky with zero murders for so long that we forgot what the real world is like." Mason knows Bill means well. Bill is a wise generous man who seems to have always been the man on the top of the mountain that Mason would confide when he was confused or needed reassurance.

"Yes but in the real world does it have four murders in such a short period of time by possibly one man? Not like Philly where they can have that in one night but by four different killers."

"True . You are a smart man just remain calm and in control. Everyone is uptight but sooner or later this will break."

"I appreciate what you are doing. I try to remain calm but it is hard." Mason changes the conversation because he can feel an uncomfortable depressed feeling."Well if it makes you feel better I am going out with Melissa this weekend. Maybe out of town so we can act like our lives are normal for at least a couple of days." He gives a light chuckle.

"There you go. Why didn't you cut me off before I ran off on a tangent?"

"It seems everyone seems to try to help me and I appreciate that and don't want to be abrupt or rude to someone and cut them off when all they are is concerned about me. Understand?" Mason asks hoping not to have been offensive in anyway.

"Absolutely. Well where are you heading now?" Bill asks realizing his point and extended hand had been recognized.

"Not sure. Crime scene, office, a neighborhood to search for clues?"

"Well good luck."

"Thanks. I will be in touch."

Mason heads out the door with his head down .He is depressed. I need to get a break he thinks to himself.

He heads out the corridor and tries not to think about the murders. He starts to think about what he can do this weekend. Maybe a bed and breakfast. Melissa always loved doing that every now and then. Who knows maybe I'll take her out in the country and go for a walk or even horseback riding. He laughs to himself .I probably won't be able to walk for a week if I do that. At least she can put her mind at ease. He knows she is stressed out for him and he wants to do whatever it takes so she can be relieved from the pressure.

He approaches the door and heads outside .Reaches in his pocket for his keys then he checks his watch for the time .He reaches his car and gets in. Pauses a second and decides it is lunchtime.

Lance decides to stop by the local Wal-mart to pick up some necessities.

He is there in five minutes. It is not far away from where he lives. He frequents there often for the oddball stuff he can't get at the grocery store. He heads in and grabs a cart .He hears people talking with words like "murder ", killing","scared" and others. He knew what the buzz would be yet he is unfazed by it. He stops to look at the magazines but he just stands there gazing at them thinking about what he hears. He feels no remorse. He then questions himself and wonders why he is doing it. As quick as it enters his head he answers his own question. He does it because he is sick of seeing people who walk on others. Those are the people who ruin other people's lives because they have the power to. He feels his job is to vindicate those who are powerless.

Power is not muscular strength. This kind of power he deals with is that the some people will never attain. The kind of power a 250 pound football doesn't have that a 110 pound man can have. Power is confidence to the hundredth degree. In some ways it is arrogance that can be abused. Like a drug too much of it can be detrimental to anyone. It can turn the most innocent, humble person into an egotistical bully. It can make a person forget who he is or where he came from. Power can be mental and that is where most people suffer and succumb to those who have it. Those people know how to use it and get what they want .They can make a person feel like shit while make themselves feel better. This is where Lance gets his motivation.

He was one of those who were powerless more then once. Being fired once with two other people so the bonus of an upper level manager could be achieved. Another was because he was a threat to a person higher then him who knew Lance was making waves with his ideas for the company. Everyone was impressed but when it seemed inevitable Lance was about to be promoted he was fired or laid off for conflict of interest as it was so stated. Knowing the reason was personal and cost him a promotion. He then saw people in the unemployment line with some similar stories. These people he felt for because Lance being single knew he could get away without a job for a short time but those who had families or had tough times in life were burden with the loss of the job unjustifiably-at least in Lance's eyes.

He then started entertaining the thoughts of revenge. He figured he would frame people but that would be too tough with no guarantee results then he one day snapped.

He was watching the news two months ago and he saw a single mom get laid off because she could make it to work one day because her child had a breathing disorder she was born with. Since it required taking time off to get an operation done and for follow ups she was fired not for using her time up but requesting additional time. She understood that it would be unpaid time off but that was not good enough. She was crying and stated how she had to return the gifts she bought her child because his birthday was so she could pay the bills. Lance snapped relating this girl to Amy from the grocery store. That following week it bugged to no end. He would drive around and take notice of the have and have nots of society. Those who were given the luxuries and those who earned them. He also realized not everybody who is a has not is unfortunate some of it is brought on by laziness and not misfortunes. He only feels for people like the woman with the child and the breathing disorder. So he thought of how to help this girl out. He wrote a check for two hundred dollars out to a fund for her. He saw her on the news three nights later. She mentioned the kindness of the public and said she hopes to get another chance at her old place of business because the benefits helped cover the costs of her child's situation. She cried pleading that they listen to her. She could not afford the Cobra plan and begged someone to help her with her company. It was then Lance came up with a plan, a plan of murder. Lance figured if he killed the person who fired her then just maybe someone who would replace him would have a sympathetic ear for her and if not well at least the bastard is dead. It was this night the Lance Grohan decided he would lay his own justice. Murder for those who wish they could. Those who wished evil upon others who had a better situation and made it apparent to those who didn't.

Yes he knew it is wrong to murder. He believes an eye for eye. Lance is not the most religious guy but he does know his religion. He has a strong faith. Yet no faith condones murder, right ? In the bible it does state an eye for eye. It does talk about on the last day the good shall enter heaven and the evil shall perish in hell .Did Cain not kill Abel? Did not the flood purpose be to kill all of the non believers of God that is why the arc was built? Lance is coming up with many reasons where death was a suitable punishment. He did not see himself as the angel form Passover or a messenger of God but this was his crusade. It felt personal because he was so passionate about it.

He tried not to think of himself like all other serial murders like Dahmer, Bundy, Ramirez but someone more like Goetz who was a vigilante back in New York subway. Yes he felt like he was losing control and yet and the same time he was completely coherent and aware to know what every thought and action he was thinking.

In a sense he would parallel himself as a Robin Hood for the weak or incapable. Doing to the wrong doers that others would only dreamed of. This is how it all started. It was that day he knew what he wanted to do.

Later that day researched the person who had her fired and started making plans on how to find the gentleman and kill him. Lance being a B+ student in college, who never studied, never really achieved academically what he was capable of but he was quite smart and cunning. He retrieved all the information he needed and two days later started tracking the gentleman's moves and then one night he made his move.

He knew the gentleman worked late to where he was typically one of the last people leaving or close to it. He followed the man out of work and when the man got to his car Lance hit him from behind. He knocked him out. Lance noticed the guy always parked under the trees far from the other vehicles so if it snowed his windows would be free from it. Lance also noticed the light falls about 25 feet short of the car so it is hard to make out shadows let alone figures. He parked his car next to the auditor's facing out on the driver's side of the auditor's. Then when the man came to his car Lance came from behind the tree with a metal pipe and hit him across the back of the head. Throwing the man in the back seat of Lance's car, he tie wraps his hands and feet. He duct tapes his mouth and puts a blanket over him as he jumps in the front seat and takes off .The seat has a tarp laid across it to prevent any stains or fibers from falling into the cracks of the seat that way he pulls it out and nothing of trace in the car to be found. One minute and flawlessly he pulls it off.

He had scoped out a vacant warehouse that had multiple entrances but at least one entrance that was hard to find when it was dark. He starts heading that way which is about 10 minutes away.

He never will forget that night .He vividly remembers the rush he had as he waited for the man to come to his car. The way he could he his heart beat and feels like it was coming through his chest. His thoughts of if he was doing the right thing or if he had what it took. Moments of doubt and weakness entered his mind. Did he have what it took? He prayed he would not cower when he came up on the man, he didn't .After he hit the man then all the doubts were gone.

He drove remembering how this is what he felt needed to be done, at least for his sake. He knows he will get caught and life as he knows it will be over but at least some victim he felt had been paid back through his actions.

He carried out his first murdered by carrying him into the warehouse and awaking the man before he was to kill him.

Funny he thinks how the person pours out all the wrongs they have done to get to this point and think they can be absolved by offering money to Lance. That is all these people think can resolve their problems. Money is the band aid that heals all wounds. Lance takes the tape off their mouths because no one can hear them where he takes them and wants to hear them repent for whatever brought them there. Just like a priest in reconciliation he holds the solution or the resolve to make things seem better and instead of the rosary it is death.

He puts the tape back over the man's mouth as he tightens the cargo straps. They get so tight that Lance starts using his leg to add leverage. The man's face pours tears as if he had walked through a waterfall. The fear in his eyes is apparent and then they open as wide as they could to the point Lance stops, thinking they are going to come out. At that moment he hears a snap and realizes the ribs are breaking and the man fights for a few seconds but there is no air getting to his lungs. He then watches the eyes roll back into his head.

It is over.

Lance leaves everything the way it is. He goes out the way he came in. He takes one last look at the scene. He takes in the moment. The whole night run through his head like an old 78 record. He did it. The feeling is that of completion, an accomplishment. He remembers that feeling just like it was yesterday. He always wears gloves, never carries anything in any pockets so nothing will fall out and can be traceable to track him down. Being meticulous is no problem for him so this part is natural maybe that is why he thinks he will never get caught.

He remembers his next murder was a female who was a real bitch to everyone. She enjoyed thinking she was the queen and was perfect yet she to him was a seriously fucked up person. He had nothing against her till she fired a guy from his gym for not kissing her ass. He heard other stories of the woman being a liar and fabricating stories to look like some innocent person. Well enough was enough one night when he heard about the firing he knew plenty of her because she trained at the same gym and watched the charade of her life and it made him sick to watch. He planned out his next murder and carried it out within 3 weeks. She lived in a town about twenty five minutes away he set it up to look like an accident inside her home. Funny no one missed her or spoke well of her when they heard she died. He felt such gratification from what he had done.

"Excuse me, sir" .Lance snaps out of his trance. "Oh I am sorry I guess I was in deep thought."

"No problem just need a newspaper." Lance backs up to let the man through. He realizes he is taking up space and decides to get the errand done.

He walks through the store, picks up some water, dog food, and soda for the house. He then decides to check out the electronic section. After checking out the mp3 players he heads towards the hardware section. He picks up some of the tools of his trade; duct tape and some tie wraps .He buys the two foot long ones and some smaller ones. He thinks if he really needs the smaller ones to himself and decides hell if he doesn't need it to kill someone he is sure he can use them around the house. This Wal-mart has the big ties wraps that usually heating and cooling suppliers would carry but he realizes he may stand out if that is all he buys there with duct tape and then a day or two later there are murders involved with those items.

He walks through the store and decides to check out. He passes a woman with three kids who are well behaved. He gets a warm good feeling .He looks forward to marrying and having children.   They are in the aisle he wants to check. She looks up at him and smiles.

"Go ahead I am in no rush "he says.

"You sure? You may want to go ahead of me they may drive you nuts if you stand there long enough." She laughs.

"No I enjoy kids. To me they are a relief. I hope mine are as good as yours when I have some."

"Thanks they have their moments so don't let them fool you." Lance looks at her and sees the happiness that her children bring her and he enjoys her company. He sees what he believes his girlfriend will be like with kids when they have them. So happy and youthful .He can't wait to go back home and see his girlfriend.

"Oops you better watch that one otherwise she may have an unnecessary sugar rush." He points at the little girl with pig tails trying to open a snickers bar. They laugh together to then be interrupted by the sound of a customer two people up front at the counter.

"Honestly are you kidding me? I have stood in an express line for almost ten minutes and then I get up to check out and you tell me your register can't accept checks? Where the hell is the god damn sign?!!" An angry average build, dark hair gentleman yells at the clerk. Dressed in an expensive suit he starts making others look over. Lance looks around and notices a sign at the beginning of the register stating " Cards or cash only".

"Uh sir I have a sign at the beginning of the register." The clerk points towards it.

The angry customer cuts past the woman and her kids. Lance is in between him and the sign as the guy tries pushing his way through.

"Excuse me." Lances says affirmatively.

The guy looks at him. "I just want to see the sign."

"Oh where exactly does it say no checks?"

"Well I did write ..."

"Don't talk back to me son. You write a freaking sign on an index card and it doesn't state 'No checks' .Now I need to tie up the line and my afternoon up for your shortcomings."

"I am sorry sir."

Don't apologize to that asshole Lance thinks. He can feel his blood boil as this guy blows up and the three kids start watching the way this guy acts.

"Hey buddy calm down there are kids around."

"You talking to me? I look like your damn buddy? You know what –"At that moment a manager interjects before the scene becomes even more distracting.

"OK can I help clear up the problem here?" A voice from the right comes. It is the store manager who comes over in a nick of time. Lance felt his face getting red with anger for the irritation this man was causing .A woman comes over and the clerk tells her the problem.

"Excuse me Mister…"

"Cleters." States the guy.

"Mr. Cleters I will process your check at another register and you can stay here and then you can go."

"About damn time." Lance watches this Cleters guy slowly backs down.

"All I need you to do is give Robert your driver's license number and home phone number."

"OK."

As Robert reaches for pen and paper, Lance pulls out his cell phone and enables memo. He starts opening a new document .He stops and waits.

The manager heads to another register and the clerk asks Mr. Cleters his info.

"Would you like to write it down sir?" As he pushes a pen and paper towards him.

"No I wouldn't that is your job."

"Ok then. Can I have your address and phone number?" Robert starts to write the information down as Mr. Cleters delivers it. As he starts Lance types the info into his cell phone and the man says it. He stops briefly to see if people are watching him plug the info into his phone. He notices no one and continues.

"3212 Pineapple Dr.-555-221-7825. Anything else?"

"No I think that will be enough hopefully will be right over so you can get out of here." Robert shoots the customer a dirty look as the customer looks for the manager. Lance meanwhile saves the information and puts it in his pocket.

"Me too. You people are pathetic. Never work for me with the laziness and incompetence I see here. That is why you are here and I am not."

Ridiculous the way this guy is treating the clerk .Other lines peer over to see the ruckus or wonder what the next asinine and ignorant thing this man will say. Lance starts to say something but the manager comes over. The manager hands the customer the receipt, wishes him off and apologizes for the inconveniences. The customer gives her a rude gesture .Lance hopes the man looks back at him and says something. The man heads out the door in a rush not looking back.

Lance knows at this moment, this man will be his next victim. Anxious to just leave and follow the guy his thoughts are interrupted by the woman.

"Some people are just so stuck on themselves. I am just happy he kept his mouth clean in front of my girls."

"Me too .I would have to step in at that point .I don't like violence but a stance had to be made with kids around."Lance thinks a point will be made in the future but in Lance's way.

The lady moves up and gets checked out .As she leaves she turns around and smiles at Lance .She wishes him a good day. He does likewise .He starts to empty his cart as his eyes follow her and her children at the door.

"You handled that well with that guy."

"Yeah I see them all but he may have been the worst. You never know what a person is made of until they open their mouth or do something stupid."

"I agree," as he pulls out his wallet for the clerk.

"Most people hide who they really are when they are out maybe this guy has no problem showing the world he is a jerk." Lance can tell Robert is irked by the way he was treated .He was embarrassed and demoralized by that guy.

"Well that is $15.44."

Lance finishes the transaction and heads out. "Have a good one."

"Couldn't get worse then it just was", states the clerk. Not for you but for Mr. Cleters it will Lance thinks to himself. He heads out towards the front and proceeds through the door .He stops immediately. A dirty man stands outside the doorway peddling for money. Lance recognizes the man and knows him too well. It is the town bum or to some, including Lance, the town crazy. Not sure of his real name people refer to him as Caveman.

He tries to head out through the door furthest from the beggar Lance is caught in the corner of Caveman's eye.

"Hey you, sir! You have some money for a homeless man?"

"No sorry I just use my credit card I carry no cash."

"Liar."

"Excuse me?!" Lance stops in his tracks and a woman bumps into him from behind." Sorry maam"

"You heard me. You have no money but I am sure you will feed your face at somewhere which only takes cash!"

"Do you want to go through this again?"

The man looks at him puzzled. Lance is referring to the last time he crossed paths with the beggar. He was leaving Wal-mart about a month ago when the same beggar approached him. Knowing of him from people talking about him at Lance's work he knows the man was a decorated Vietnam Veteran who served two tours maybe two tours too many according to some.

He has no family in the area and any family outside the state have not kept in touch with him. He lost his job due to his paranoia and skitzing out at work which was scaring people .He went to a doctor but his medical coverage would only cover a percentage and he couldn't afford the rest along with the medicine so he stopped going. He eventually couldn't keep up with his mortgage from the loss of his job and then his unemployment timed out. At that point he lost his house and lived at a local shelter for a year or two. He was troublesome there due to his problems. He was then kicked out and has lived on the streets since. He has a violent streak when he has a bad day begging for money. People have had the cops called on him .Lance was one of those people at the other end of a tantrum. He told the beggar he had no money, then the man grabbed his arm and threaten him and told him he better not see him come out with any items and not have any money for him. When Lance pulled away from him the gentleman grabbed again this time with force and reached in his pocket but before he could grab whatever it was he wanted, Lance threw up against the wall and a scuffle ensued. Cops came out, took the man away and released him later that day.

It was there at the police station where he learned about the man's past. Lance actually does feel moved for the man but he can't accept he constant nagging and pandering the guy does. It is one thing to ask for money and another to try to force it out of someone. Why does Wal-mart just not remove him from there? He is not the Salvation Army.

"Oh I remember you, you tried to hurt me and when I was about to kick your ass before the cops came."

"Yes old man that was me. So we are not going to do that again right? "says Lance with a sarcastic tone almost hoping for the man to get smart back with him.

The man looks at him and says nothing. He walks towards the other entrance and bugs a couple heading in to the store. Lance stands and briefly watches. Usually being a man for the less unfortunate it is different here. He feels those who have no home but not for those who make it uncomfortable for other people. Sometimes angry when he sees the beggar at the front of the store he wants to turn around and come back another time.

Lance heads towards his car deciding where he is going to eat lunch. Hey maybe he will take the beggar up on his idea. He thinks Wendy's or Burger King. They are across the street from each other. The whopper sounds appealing he decides so Burger King it is and pulls out in that direction.

Mason leaves the coroner's office with nothing that will help him out. He thinks to himself how nothing is changing for him. No clues .Nothing he already didn't know. He heads back to the crime scene from last night. Something has to pop up .Four murders and no clues? This only happens in the movies with this many killings. He gets back in his car .It is 1215 and it is lunch time. He drives towards the crime scene and passes a Wawa .He contemplates stopping but he is hungry for a burger and there is a Burger King on the way. Within a couple of minutes he drives towards the Burger King and changes his mind. He decides to go to Wendy's. He pulls into the lot and heads in .He orders a triple and normally avoids the heart attack burger but there are bigger things on his mind today. He gets his order and picks a booth towards the window but away from the crowd.

He grabs the local newspaper on the tables at the booth next to him. Headline states in bold print "Serial Murderer?" Cops won't say." He continues reading the paper. He reads the different scenarios the reporters point out hoping it will jog his memory and maybe help him brainstorm. Nothing in the paper helps him. All the information is basically useless.

He just keeps eating his burger. A brief moment of happiness overcomes him thinking how he calls this the heart attack burger to his girlfriend and how she would laugh. It would make him happy. Her smile always did that for him.

He wonders why he even reads the paper. It has no new information. He should know since he tells them the information. He hears a horn outside, looks and sees an Explorer blasting its horn because someone cut in front of him. Thank God he thinks to himself his luck he would have to do an accident report.

"Excuse me, Mason?"

Mason quickly looks to his left and sees a woman standing at his table. Dressed in a nice long black coat, shoulder length brown hair and fairly attractive he wipes his mouth.

"Hi, Can I help you? Sorry I do not recognize you."

"That is ok you don't know me. I was hoping to steal a few minutes of your time .May I?" she gestures her hand to the seat across from him asking for permission to sit with him.

"Yeah sure go right ahead. How can I help you?"

She sits down and loosens her jacket.

"My name is Marie Cantor. I have been following the murders and you seem to be the person who people should come to."

"Yes you are correct with that." Mason starts to sit up more attentively now. Could this be the break I need? A person who has a lead or knows someone or something? Or this someone who is just going to ask the same questions reporters asks? Mason can feel a rush coming on. Or maybe this is just a person who needs their personal security elevated. Well whichever she has his attention.

"Well Mr. Kade".

"Mason, please."

"I do not know you and feel to call you by your first name like a friend or family member is inappropriate. I come to you with respect. You understand?"

"Yeah sure, go on." Mason replies a little puzzled.

"Mr. Kade, these murders, four of them they are related. There is no suicide or unrelated murders .You know that Mr. Kade and I do too." Mason looks at her and now starts to get an uneasy feeling.

"These are all connected like a puzzle. This stuff does not happen in a town like this and not be related in a couple month window. I don't believe you are trying to fool people and please Mr. Kade. Don't. You will lose those who believe in you. Just because you don't see them or talk them don't mean they are not there."

"Ok hold on one second Marie .I mean Ms Cantor .Miss is that correct?"

"Yes but you can call me Marie. Just because I believe in a way a person should be treated doesn't mean you have to. I understand and accept I maybe different then most but I am like them too .Good."

"Ok then Marie. I have a few questions before you go on because I think I am getting lost right now. I am not trying to lie to anyone about these cases. I tell as much as I can without giving away anything that will help the case. So what you hear is pretty much the truth. Second who are these people that trust me I don't know or don't hear from? I am lost."

"Mr. Kade. People like me. Who read the newspaper, watch TV and care about what is going on in the world let alone our town .We care about what is happening and want to help but only those who are trusting. Telling people the cases are not related is a lie. Then they look at you and it makes it seem you are bewildered. Do not be a snake oil salesman Mr. Kade. You can affect more then you know if you do it right."

Mason sits back and can not make of this conversation what is going on This Mr. Kade stuff is starting to bug him but he does not want to be rude she must be like 30 years old and yet is so –proper. She definitely seems like one of a kind. Maybe she just goes to church a lot, like everyday.

Is she telling me something almost like subliminally? Is she the killer and knows playing some kind of game? Maybe she is just crazier then the killer?

Or maybe she is scared and is at wits end. Mason develops more questions as she talks .She talks in a soft but very stern voice. If she had a stick she would be hitting me with it to drive whatever her point is home. As she speaks he can hear the Twilight theme going in the background.

She leans towards him and starts speaking again.

"You will make the others so happy and at ease. It hurts me to see this. I hoped to let you know and you can do what is right. That is one reason I am here."

"One reason?"

"Yes Mr. Kade. Actually it is the second reason I am here .The first is I am here to help you with these murders. There will be more deaths and I want to help."

Mason's face becomes blank.

"How can you help? More deaths?"

"Yes .More."

"Ok without being rude .What the hell are you talking about? How do you know there will be more deaths?"

There is a pause between them and she looks at him with a dead stare and says"I can see the future."

Mason wants to laugh.

"Oh you can? Will I hit the lottery tonight?" he says sarcastically.

"I do not appreciate your sarcasm. I came to you with respect and would like it reciprocated back. I don't expect you to believe me but the future is like a book. It is already written. The only difference between me and you is I have already seen the book. You have to wait till it to comes to know what happens. Then and only then maybe you may give me some due."

"I am sorry. Seriously though you have to look at it my way .I have four murders not many leads and then you come up to me with all these people and this stuff about seeing the future Which by the way you said people want to help me and support me but then you said the others would be happy and at ease. Wouldn't that be assumed if we caught the killer?"

"No, not them Mr. Kade."

"Huh? Who then?"

"The victims. They can rest in peace once it is over."

Mason thinks to himself .I should have seen this coming from a mile away. He is dumbfounded and feels blindsided. Almost like she had him hypnotized all this time and then released him from it by telling him about the victims.

"You are now telling me you talk to dead people?" he barks out loud enough to draw the attention to them by people sitting nearby.

"No, I just listen", she says softly trying to calm him down and avoiding a scene.

"Oh well that clears it up .I thought you were just crazy all this time." Mason's face gets flush from the anger." I have sat here gave you my time and in about fifteen minutes you wasted my time. I will keep you in mind when I need to talk to my dog that passed away last month..."

"Enough!" Marie blurts out." I will not tolerate your ignorance. I have a gift that you will never understand .but mark my words Mr. Kade, the murders will pick up in frequency in the next couple of weeks. You will get help that is needed but yet unaccommodating. You strength, will and beliefs will be tested. You will question what you believe in and trust things you doubted. You will close the door to your faith .Open those of fear and disparity .Your body and heart will grow heavy while your legs grow thin. Then you will see what has always been there .I can lead you to the light but I can't open your eyes."

"Well when that happens I will keep you in mind." He starts to clean up his area he is disgusted. He tries to get away from everything for just 15 minutes and look at what happens. He finishes off his soda as he listens to her. He has lost his appetite. He tries to signal to her by his actions that he has had enough.

"Oh you will. You will have a sign. Remember this, when is a book not a book? "

Mason sits stunned at her speech and slouches back.

"I am sorry."He gets up and starts to put his jacket on.

"I am here every Thursday around this time .I will help you .Otherwise may God be with you Mr. Kade."

"Take care Marie."

Mason heads towards the trash can and dumps his trash. He grabs his keys and heads out the door angry, confused and rushed. This has thrown him off but hell she is crazy .I have to worry about one crazy person right now and he is killing people. She is harmless-and useless. He gets in the vehicle and starts to crank some music as he pulls away.

He is angry but not sure at what. Maybe that he wasted his time listening to her. Maybe she knew they were trying to mislead the public or worse yet maybe she knew they were clueless at who was doing this. Whatever the reason he could feel perturbed.

He just wants to get away, get a break but in all likelihood that won't be happening till the case is solved. Wouldn't look right. Well one thing is fir sure, she was a weird one. He takes a left on Main St and stops at the light.

He decides he will stop by the crime scene and see if anything was overlooked that may help him out. After that stop by the station and look over some of the evidence .It shouldn't take long since there is really nothing worth looking at.

       Lance heads towards his house from Burger King take out and figures out his agenda for the day. Jill doesn't get up till about 2:30 to 3 pm so he has about two to three hours or so to kill. He realizes the phone number in his cell phone from the asshole at the Wal-Mart . There you go he thinks to himself. You have some homework to do. He arrives home and unpacks his whopper meal. He sits down at the television in the living room and starts eating .He passes by the news .Hell ,he thinks, I already know there was a murder last night do I need to keep seeing it? It is Thursday and all the football on is just rerun of last weeks games or previews for the upcoming week. Maybe something good is on the A&E channel. He stops there but nothing interests him .He was hoping a documentary about a serial murderer or a mystery of some type was on. He always like a good movie or show to keep the mind occupied. I should have rented a movie when I was out .A few good ones have just been released .Oh well I am not running out now. Too bad I have no movie channels but they are a year behind and I am not going to wait a year when I can go to it when it comes out or a few months till hits DVD. I am sure something will pop up hopefully before I am done my lunch. Flipping through the channels he pauses at a rerun of CSI. Cool. Being one of his favorite shows this will do the trick .Even if he has seen it already he has no problem watching it again. He finishes up his meal as he watches the show. He leans back during a commercial and thinks what is next for the day. The show comes back on and his attention is diverted back to the show. It is the episode where Grissom catches a killer by the food found in his pet pirahana's belly. Feeding the victim to your pet fish that is something I never thought of. Do goldfish chow down on humans? He has three goldfish Larry, Moe, Curly and envisions them nibbling on his fingers. He chuckles as the show comes to an end. Maybe these guys, referring to the town police, need Grissom and gang to help them out.

       He gets up throws his trash away and cleans up after himself .Afterwards he checks on his girlfriend. He ponders slipping under the covers with her and waking her up only his way of knowing. Twice in one day would be nice. It has been awhile since that happened and besides he needs the exercise he thinks. Ha, ha. He pushes the door open and thinks well maybe she will be grumpy and kill any shot of anything happening that day or night. Hmmmnn. I have no whip cream here right now anyway. Nah, he stops and heads away from the bedroom, back towards the couch where he lays down and turns the television off. He closes his eyes, let's his mind drift off .He wonders if he will ever get caught with the murders since he just did one last night. Sometimes he gets an uneasy feeling when he thinks about the murders. A paranoia that plays with his mind till he goes through the whole episode again is his head and convinces himself he was flawless. Still, regardless what mood he is in he wonders will he get sloppy with the more he does.

He switches his thoughts from discomfort.

He feels justified in his actions that someone else's life may be more peaceful. He knows it won't be for a few days at the shortest if he was to act on anything. He feels a rush coming on not from the thought of killing a man but the thought of killing a man who deserves it. Honestly how many more people will be happy if this man is out of their life, he wonders. The guy in Wal-mart has really irritated him. No one can act like that in a store and be the complete opposite outside of it. He must be pretty much an asshole to most. Sooner or later some reporter will print and actually almost thank me for killing someone he or the public in general disliked. Right now he has killed no one who does not have a big impact on the public but that will change shortly.

He ponders when will he stop? Tomorrow? After this guy? Another ten guys? Does it matter? Sure there are some sad families but they have to in their most loneliness of times actually say "That ass had it coming to him."

He believes everyone wishes evil but it only differs on how evil they wish upon someone. So he is the person who does the evil no one else would try to do. He tries to think of the name of the movie where a robber goes and robs the banks but destroys the original documents of the debts people owe to the banks. At first the public sees him as a criminal but after they see no one gets hurt in the bank they realize he is just helping them get something for free and they starting cheering for him .They read the newspaper and hope their bank gets hit so they have a chance of getting out of the debt they owe. When people realize that something can actually make their life easier or better but it is wrong then they start trying to compromising their beliefs to justify a wrong. Hell maybe I can a good nickname like all the famous serial murderers, he thinks. Yet I don't want to be seen like them because I am different. I just don't go around and kill innocent people .These people needed to be punished and they are well past getting scolded. I kill the Ebenezer Scrooges of the world.

I want people to think "Am I the type of person that could be next? Will I be the target of that serial murderer?" That is what should go through their mind. The same paranoia that the Son of Sam or the Zodiac Killer did. People did not want to go out or were worried that their sign was the next sign to be targeted. A sickness that they were living their last moments. Yes that is what I want.

Fear.

If they were not these people then they had nothing to fear BUT they had to know it. Someone will eventually figure out the link between these victims if not then there will be lots of dead bodies.

He thinks about the rush he gets from killing a person. He doesn't see the life he takes from a person like a normal person would. He sees it as if he is the angel of death just like the Angel of Passover going from door to door striking those who were not marked. He goes from town to town stealing the breath from people who did not protect themselves from the angel of death. Now though it is a different story. Now it is getting out there someone is snatching people's lives from them. They don't know why. Lance grins he has the power to control a town. Funny this is what he kills people for abusing. He doesn't abuse it though just like using a pump if you inflate something too much then you destroy it. He knows how to use his power of fear. The only thing he hopes is that the people understand why they are being picked. It would make his job so much easier when they understand why. Well considering the police in this town are pretty much in over their heads I guess I am going to have to wait till the big boys are called in. Maybe then they will have some profilers get involved then come up with some warped profile of Lance. A forty year old guy, who has no life lives with his mom, is a loner. You know the typical profile for everyone they can't figure out. Just like the locals try to doing things the big boys do with news conferences and false information they are putting out there to draw me out is a joke. Lance thinks there is no way I will call them and what have them trace or play it on television where someone recognizes his voice? Hell no I am not falling for that. The more anonymous the better. I don't want a face put to the fear. It is much scarier when you do not know when or where it will strike. No rhyme or reason.

I want them to breathe it, eat it, piss it out. I want to be the reason they change their attitude. The reason they think twice about having God complexes, talking down to someone or ruining someone's life. No one is above someone because of a title of a boss. Their blood is no different then mine. What? They go to school and that makes them a better person. What does school do for some? Teach them how to boss people around? Elevate themselves so it is easier to demean or look down and sympathizes at a person's life because it is not as enriched as their own? Those are the bastards that need an attitude adjustment.

Only God can pass judgment on who is worthy or not .Even then it is not the same judgment people think they have the power of doing. A priest can not pass judgment on someone's life .They see everyone unbiased .They hear their sins and they help them repent. Regardless if they murdered someone or just stolen a pack of gum .They do not condemn. They know they are the buffer, do gooder to make the soul right for God when the day of reckoning comes upon and then and only then will true judgment or damnation shall be given. If they can't condemn or look down on people as they as considered so close to God then how do these average Joes think they can do it?

Consequences. That is the problem nowadays there is no consequences or punishments .People can act like whatever they want and walk all over others. Too big for their britches. Well that shit is done with me, Lance thinks.

Whatever happen to respect he wonders? My parents would have never talked to someone the way these younger generation kids act.

Somewhere every kid that grew up decided that they would be easier on their kids then their parents because they were so tough. Then that line you would have never crossed as a kid with your parent is now almost crossed everyday. Hell he remembers being at the mall and some fifteen year old kid was cursing at his parents. The parents had no reaction so obviously it was normal for this for him. Now back then your dad would have knocked out half your teeth for something like that. Everyone wants to be the kid's friend and forget about the parenting .Why? Probably because a parent has to be tough with a kid but a friend doesn't need to yell. Oh well screw it.

Everything comes around it is just a matter of time. Just like clothes or fads that are out 10 years ago then it comes back. This will happen again I am sure but total anarchy will rear its ugly head first.

Lance yawns and he can feel a weariness coming on and a few minutes later, he drifts off into a sleep.

He gets up notices he had drifted off for about an hour or two. It is almost 330 and she is still asleep. I guess I could get dinner started or even thought about. Steak sounds good tonight. Checks over the fridge and everything seems to be there that would be needed. Oops no ketchup. Ok that now just required another run. What good is a refrigerator without ketchup?

Lance is a ketchup fiend. You name it, it gets ketchup. Just as sacred to him as a person's house keys he would stop anything he is doing to make sure he has his ketchup. So he grabs his jacket and keys. He proceeds towards the door and heads out.

He closes the door.

Gotta have that ketchup—and oh yeah don't forget the whip cream.

It is Friday night and Lance is getting out of the shower. Jill is straightening up the house since her friends are coming over for a Longeberger basket and candle party. Lance plans on working on the computer or tiding up the office in the basement.

He gets in the bedroom and gets his clothes on.

"Hey babe?"

"Yes hun?"

"How long will they be here tonight?"

"Like till 11 or midnight and you know Kara she will make herself at home and tell me about the neighborhood .You know who is doing what and what everyone makes."

"Oh great. How did I forget about Kara? Well I will be on the computer so if you need me you know where I will be. Just don't ask me if you can spend eighty dollars on a basket to hold the keys."

"Ok honey I won't. I'll just buy it. "

"Oh you will huh?"

"Yeah I'll make it worth it though." She winks at him with an evil smile.

"Oh you will." Lance laughs reconfirming what she said.

"They should start getting here in the next twenty minutes or so. I told them to start arriving around 830."

"Do you need anything? I am going to head down if you don't."

"No I am fine thanks honey."

"You know where I will be."

Lance heads down the steps and stops in the kitchen to grab a drink and his cell phone.

He enters the office and closes the door behind him. Ahh peace, he thinks to himself. He turns on the monitor and scans his computer for some to music to listen to. He turns on some U2 to start. He reaches for his cell phone and scrolls for some information.

"There it is." He looks at the screen.

"Ok Mr. Cleters where do you live?

He enters the address and studies the screen. Since Lance is well learned in computers and has skills to actually do some simple hacking he has software to dig up personal information that the average person does not have access to. He does some searches and finds what he needs.

"There we go" .He prints out the page. "You are next." He has a feeling come upon him almost like a rush of excitement.

He looks over the page. He contemplates where and when he will punish Charles Cleters.

He hears people starting to come in upstairs .He walks out of the office and into another room to play his Playstation .A hour goes by, he heads upstairs and walks into the kitchen where he pokes his head into the living room and notices a full house. It is 830 pm.

"Excuse me waiter?" a cheerful female voice blurts out.

"Damn it, snagged" Lance laughs out

."Did you think you were going to get by me Lance?"

"No Kara .They should have just sent you to find Osama he would have had no chance."

Everyone laughs in the room. There are about twelve ladies in the room.

"Jill seems to be on a shopping spree. You are such a sweet guy to encourage her to do this." The room fills with laughter.

"Yes I believe all men will look at me as a role model for letting their woman spends $50 on a basket for bananas. I am sure all the guys will invite me over their houses."

"Sure they will" Kara says with a smile.

"Well you ladies enjoy yourself I am going out to take care of some important matters then it is back into my cave figure how much overtime this night will cost me."

A few see yas come from the gathering and Lance heads out.

The women pour some drinks and continue their party.

A few hours pass by and Lance comes in. He peeps in towards the living room and back into the kitchen where he gets a drink. It is midnight when he decides to go up to bed and watch TV till he doses off. As he goes upstairs he says his goodnights to the 4 women left including Jill. She tells him she only spent sixty five dollars on a basket and candle. Wow he thinks to himself not too bad. He gives her a kiss on the head and tells her to enjoy herself he is going up.

After about forty five minutes of television he drifts off to sleep and Jill comes up five minutes later trying to be quiet as she can knowing her man had a long day.

It is about 830 am and Jill wrestles around the bed grabbing the covers.

"What are you doing?" asks Lance.

"Trying to keep warm you big hog."

"Hog?" he laughs.

"Where did you go last night?" she asks.

"I told you I had some stuff to do."

"Oh till 11?"

"Yep" he responds.

"I hope these matters are not female."

"No babe."

"Good because I was going to get out of bed and make you breakfast if you were nice to me BUT..."

"I was being nice. You know I love you and want to be your slave, worship you and everything you do .What else could I want?"

"Ok you big ass kiss I was going to do it for you anyways. What do you want?"

"What are you going to have?"

"I was thinking about eggs and some bacon maybe hash browns."

Lance thinks briefly." That sounds good to me. Need a hand?"

"No I am fine. My treat. Stay here I'll bring it up to you when it is done."

"WOW. Breakfast in bed, you are the best. I love you." He says with a big smile.

"I know you do." She jumps out of bed and grabs her robe and heads downstairs to start breakfast. Lance digs into the bed and smiles .Jill makes him so happy .The thought of being fed in bed also may have something to do with that he chuckles. Regardless she is a great woman and he knows he won't let her get away.

Jill starts getting the pan ready and puts butter in it to warm it up. She goes outside and gets the paper. She brings it in. She throws the eggs in the pan and while they start to cook she opens up the paper.

The headline says" Chipper found dead. " Underneath that it says "Another one?"

Jill shakes her head, I hope not she thinks to herself she starts to read the article but hears the eggs crackling. She puts it down and tends to them. She gets loss in making the breakfast and throws the paper on the pile of junk .She has more important things on her mind instead of reading about some psycho.

Meanwhile on the other side of town, Mason comes flying into the parking lot of the station after reading the paper of another murder the previous night. He had the night off, no one called him and let him know of the murder .He called in and found out everyone is at the station. He is livid. This is his case and if it is related why was he not notified?

He notices a few black SUVs parked out front and the media also outside waiting for him. The lot is like a zoo.

He gets out of his vehicle and the press rushes at him.

"Mason, is this the work of the serial murderer? They say you weren't even there. Where were you?"

"No comment .When we have something to say we will fill you in." Mason has no clue why he is out of the loop and just wants to find out what is going on.

"Is it true the Feds are now in charge?"

Mason ignores the reporter and walks through the doors. He glances back at the lot and notices how full it is but not of police cars and the media but of black SUVs and Cadillacs. The feds are here. He now has a sunken feeling in his stomach like that of the triple burger he had yesterday at lunch. Many thoughts run through his head. Will he be pulled off the case? Will the local force be embarrassed by the Feds actions or the point that they are even here?

Ok get a hold of yourself he thinks to himself .Something positive can come out of this. These guys maybe what they need but wasn't just a couple of days ago this seemed like a far fetched scenario. They must have been paying attention all the time. This murder last night must have been the straw that broke the camel's back. Maybe the feds responded to the murder last night and that is the reason for no call.

He heads towards the conference room and is redirected by the captain.

"Mace, come here into my office first."

He heads towards the office of the captains .He sees a couple of men in suit and ties standing there. God this must be the feds, he thinks to himself.

Now this is where they break the bad news to him .The feds were called in last night and he is no longer a part of the case and that is why is out in the dark now. He can fell his heart race with anger.

He walks into the captain's office. And closes the door.

"Mace, I wanted to talked to you before the briefing and fill you in. I know you are pissed off but you need to hear what is going on before you blow a gasket. Ok?"

Biting his tongue Mason reluctantly answers."Go on then."

"Ok first these gentlemen are from the FBI. I know you are not surprised. These guys were planning on coming out this week anyways and last night just pushed up the time. Which leads me to the reason you were not notified of the murder...?" The captain pulls his chair out and sits down while the two agents grab the two chairs closest to them which leaves him one chair left. Ron's body language is awkward .He is uncomfortable telling Mason what and why this is happening. Mason thinks then maybe there is more bad news that Mason is unaware of.

"Please sit down Mason." As he gestures towards the last chair. Mason sits down in it and leans forward like a cat waiting to pounce on a bird.

"Now I did not call you because I knew for two days these guys were coming out within the week and felt if I told you this it would place more pressure on you that was unwarranted. Well last night when another homicide was called in these guys decided last night was the night to come. They have come to help and give us whatever we need. The murder last night looks like he struck again. No offense to you and the station but I think we need the help. We are not prepared for someone of this caliber. I hope you understand."

Mason looks down at the ground and digests everything he has heard. He has many questions about the feds, the murder and what is next .He doesn't know where to start .He takes a deep breath and looks at Ron in the eyes.

"Cap I understand but am I in charge? I still am a part of this case right? I believe regardless murder or no murder I should have had a hint of them coming out .No offense would have been taken but I am thrown off a little by all these surprises."

"I am sorry Mason. The FBI will be leads in this but you are still on top of the food chain of info. This weekend they will be bringing more agents in and that should make it a quiet weekend for you. After all this you need it now more then ever." Ron looks at the agents. The agents sit there quietly and respectfully not interrupting the conversation.

"Well there is nothing I can do about this but get this resolved ASAP. "

"Great. I knew I could count on you to take handle with professionalism. Now Mason this is agent Mitchell Rakers he will be working with you till we catch this bastard. These guys are not going to tell you your job but help make it easier. This here his Agent Thomas Chrith he will be doing all the behind the scenes work with the FBI while you two are out on the road."

Mason looks at the agents .Mitchell is a taller leaner gentleman with intense look. So this I guess is my partner now, he thinks to himself. He offers his hand towards the agents.

"How are you?"

"Good, hopefully we make this a quick job and let you get back to a normal life." Says Mitchell is a serious tone. The other agent shakes Mason's hand and nods with a smile.

"Listen, Mason. The FBI has been watching these murders from the first double a couple of months back and it was inevitable we would be coming out when more happened. We were working another serial murder at the time, caught a break and resolved in a week which delayed us by not getting here quicker. Now would us being here helped solved it and avoided the murder last night? No probably not but maybe forensics or something may have helped slow this madman down."

"Speaking of this murder was there anything like clues or hints found." Mason asks since he is in the dark about the most recent murder.

Mitchell looks at Ron and Ron addresses the question.

"Last night nothing was found again .Now we still have the coroner's report and the feds have their forensics there as we speak so hopefully something pops up."

"Also Mason Quantico is at our disposal. Anything we need men, equipment, anything will be sent ASAP. Now I suggest you wait for the briefing which we are late for before we go into the spew and if there are more questions well I am at your service." He speaks in a tone of confidence like he knows they will catch him. He gets up and so does the rest of the room. Mason looks towards the conference room where eyes peer over to see what the delay is. Mason knows their meeting is over for now and the important stuff needs to be addressed.

"I agree let's head over."

As the agents lead and head towards the room Mason faces Ron shakes his hand to let him know everything is fine. He follows the agents into the briefing room, takes a spot at the front with them and the captain. Hopefully no one asks him questions about last night but is sure everyone knows what is going on. He looks over and sees Ron head to the podium. He sees some state cops there along with the entire local force .The third shift stayed around hoping to hear something optimistic he is sure.

"Ok people this is going to be brief and to the point. I have not much to say .We all know what happened last night. We know our serial murderer has struck. Now what you don't know is that the FBI has sent agents to help us on and off the field. Agent Mitchell Rakers will be working with Mason so if you have questions you can ask both. Now I will let the FBI do the talking." Ron steps to the side and lets the agent step up.

"Morning everyone my name is Agent Mitchell Rakers and this is Agent Thomas Chrith. I am going to be working with Mason in the field and Agent Thomas will be back he doing everything he can here. We are not here to boss you around. We are here to help catch a serial murderer."

He speaks with authority, almost an urgency. Hopefully he can help them find something to stop this maniac.

"We planned on coming out here a couple of weeks ago but something else came up and after last night's murder we knew the timetable had to be pushed up."

"A little about myself that I feel is important to know. I went four years of college for the bureau and have special training in profiling. I have worked on about 10 different serial murderer cases that local enforcement called us in for. I was part of the Funnyface killer case. For those of you who are not familiar with the case it took five years to catch the killer .He killed only five people but it was the FBI's most wanted person for that time."

"Five years to catch him? I hope that is not the time frame we have we. Right?" asks one of the local officers.

"No this person here was in the military and away when we would get out in the field to catch him. He would murder right before he would go on leave then when we was around he stay secluded and unnoticed by society."

"The FBI goal is never to let a case go on forever. As you know it does nothing good for society even if the murders stop and the evidence and witness become more damaged as time drags on. Having a murderer walking around free and giving the perception we are casually working on it is inappropriate and not good. This is not a lecture you know your jobs. We are here to add to your force with man power, technology and ideas and together we want to catch this killer before he kills again." Mitchell looks across the room trying to make eye contact with everyone to give them the reassurance this guy will be caught. He can tell that some do not believe.

"That is all I have .I just wanted to know the faces with the names you will be hearing. Now I will leave this forum open for questions. I am sure you have them so shoot."

"I have a couple of questions .I hope you don't mind." Asks another officer.

"No go ahead."

"Why did the FBI keep you on a case of one murder a year? What made the FBI get involved after the first one? Finally and probably the least important why was he called the Funnyface Killer?"

"This case may not have been heard here because it was out on the West Coast the murders. I got involved because they needed the murderer profiled so I was sent out. Then I can answer all the other questions with the following." Mitchell looks at their faces some look like children waiting for a piece of candy while others look reluctant to listen. He can tell by their expressions some of them never seen or experience what is happening or being told. Some of them may have forgotten some of the films they saw in trainings of these situations. Well they need to be prepared for the future so he continues. He turns on the projector which they brought because he wanted them to understand serial murders happen anywhere and they can be resolved regardless of the size of the town, and clicks to the photos from the Funnyface killer.

"He was called the Funnyface killer because he'd slice his victims from corners of their mouths to their ear and make faces with them." As he tells them he clicks to a picture where only the strongest of stomachs cannot be turned. "In one situation he pulled the skin of their face up and over the top of their head. "

He hears a couple of groans. He looks over at Mason who looks at the picture and takes a long look and a swallows hard. Agent Rakers then flips to a picture where the person's tongue is pulled all the way out and rests on the person's chest almost like a clown's tie. More "Oh my God's" and groans. He doesn't sit on that picture too long for he goes into the next one.

"That is not it. He then would behead them and put their heads out on the front of the property the porch or post for everyone to see. We did catch him after the fifth one when a relative saw pictures of the victims in the killer's house and notified us. When we caught him he was to leave the next week which we felt saved another life."

He looks around and knows he could be there all day telling stories but decides to get back to the topic.

"Ok now back to the matter at hand. From this moment on nothing changes with our jobs. We work like before these murders started. We ticket speeders those parked illegally. Those disturbing the peace .We may catch our murderer by not even planning it .Remember the Son of Sam was caught by a parking ticket. Anything that looks suspicious let me know who knows where it may lead."

"OK I do not want to waste anymore time. When you go out there be careful of the media .No comment to the media on everything. What I know of this case there is not much to say but what we do find about his guy should be kept quiet unless otherwise stated. The FBI needs to see everything from the scenes to the evidence before I can even give you a profile .There will be no open forum today but there will be one within the next few days. Good luck. "

With that the front of the room empties back to the captain's office while the officers disperse.

The four men gather back in the office and shut the door.

"Well Mitchell what do we say to the media. They know you are here and I am sure this is going to blow up."

"This is what we say. We are now aware there is a serial murderer. We are following up some leads and can't give any information due to the sensitivity of this case. We want the public to do everything they normally do if none of this was happening and if something looks suspicious to give the police a call. We want to emphasize this since the clues are slim from what I read."

Mason interjects." I absolutely agree on everything you said. "He looks at Ron."Cap when can I head over to the scene from last night?"

"I was going to suggest today you and the agents head there. After that then go back to other scenes or whatever they ask of you."

"Ok great. What do you guys want to do?"

"Well give us a half hour to look at some of the notes before we head out in case something interests us from elsewhere. Anything you want to say Agent Crith?"

"Not really but I want to see any physical evidence as little as it may be."

"I will take them down to evidence and bring the files there and do everything from there. Just follow me. Hey Cap you gonna talk to the media?"

"Oh wow that reminds soon we will be having schedule meetings with the media. It works much better this way. Then we can head in and out without having to stop every time to answer questions. Trust me you give them the time they somewhat make it a little easier. I am sure since this is the first serial murder in this town let alone area a lot of outlets will be here." Mitchell reaches for his briefcase and makes his way towards the door.

"That is fine. Do you suggest I just talk to them now and maybe schedule them every other day or until some information becomes available?"

"That is good. Today though we will acknowledge there is a serial murderer. We give them no clue we are in the dark but actually studying important leads which if given out could tamper with the investigation." adds Agent Chrith who is relatively quiet.

"Good idea Tom. We will work this like the Funnyface case."

Mitchell looks at Mason and states they are ready. They head out of the room towards evidence which is downstairs as they walk through the hallways there is a silence amongst them. Officers look worried or preoccupied. They look towards the lobby and see the media being led out. The lobby is too small for these crowds and people are having trouble trying to get in. As Mason leads them downstairs he thinks if he ever seen the station so flooded with people regardless for good or bad. He feels slightly overwhelmed but the agents seem so calm and assured. Mason hopes that with what they bring they can resolve this quickly.

They get to the room and set up the files on the boards and tables.

"This from here on is where we work from only stuff that leaves this room is by one of us. Tom set up the pictures on the boards. Mason if you can bring in the physical evidence and set it up on the tables that would be great. "

"No problem. I'll be back in about 5 minutes or so till I sign it out and make sure I have everything." Mason heads towards a door in the rear of the room where the evidence is stored.

"It is nice this room is so big. We can layout a lot of stuff." Tom states as he starts organizing the pics for the boards. Mason walks out of the room and goes to the office where he will grab all the case files.

Tom looks back at Mitchell. "So what do you think?"

"About what?"

"The officers. The case. Everything"

"I think they are competent enough but not experienced to know clues when they come across them. Did you see their faces when I talked about that case?"

"Funnyface?"

"Yes."

"I saw them .Did you think that was a good thing to do? You know show them something so well, raw?" Agent Crith asks politely not trying to offend Agent Rakers.

"Well Tom if they can't handle pictures then they will not do us any good out there if this killer keeps being creative."

Agent Crith then interjects. "Yes and we need to get a feel of what we are working with. We already know the killer can handle this which helps us get his mindset."

"Yeah they were almost scared to listen."

"That and they were almost caught up in the story. I hope this does not happen to them when they are out there and try to become the story."

"True but Ron and Mason seem fine."

"Yeah I like Mason he pays attention to details .I was reading a file he filled out and it was quite thorough. Usually I have questions to ask but after reading his I was pretty well informed. By the way I don't think I would want to tie up with him. He is a big boy."

"Yep looks like he touched a weight or two." Tom laughs.

"Wow did you see some of these pics?" Tom is flipping through the pictures taken back by the images he sees.

"Briefly" as Mitchell hangs some papers he glimpses over at Tom.

"This guy seems pretty sick. I am not sure what is trying to say with the way he murders like the woman with her hair pulled through the hole in the back of her head."

"From what I have read at our briefing on the way here and at Quantico. I believe from what little I know he releases his anger through his methods of killing. So much hatred we need to profile this guy quick. Get all we know and see if we can come up with something. Maybe someone who had a traumatic event recently. He may just dislike people and something is instigating him into becoming more and more through every murder."

"It seems like it is art to him. No two murders the same, a creativity in a perverse way. Do you think he is trying to outdo himself each time? We are assuming it has to be a serious crisis to bring this out." Asks Tom as he hands a Mitchell a group of pictures.

"Well Tom, looking for someone who had a crisis? To be honest how exactly does that narrow anything down? I am sure almost every other person in this town knows someone who has had an experience that can be influential."

"Yes but influential enough to kill four people?" Mitch asks looking a Tom with a look of doubt .He his overlooking some notes taken from the last couple murders.

"Do you think these are personal or random?" Tom asks as he starts organizing the some of the files.

"Not sure I need to look over everything. Did he kill the others the same way?"

As Tom is about to answer Mason walks in with a box.

"Well here is the rest of it. Find anything?"

Mitchell starts looking over everything.

"No just starting to look it over now. He kills in a different way each time it looks like right?" He holds a picture of the first victim.

"Yes and never leaves a clue. He either cleans up or wears gloves."

"Well how about we wait about these clues till we get our teams in there. We have equipment that should be able to draw something up. This is the FBI."

"Oh I am aware where you are from. You think that equipment can pick up fibers or trace that ours didn't?"

"Very possible." Mitchell answers with a sense of arrogance.

"What if we don't come up with anymore evidence?" Mason asks but trying not to sound pessimistic.

"Hey Mason," interjects Tom." Don't start giving up before we even get there. You will be amazed what we will come up with even after a site has been thoroughly searched."

"Sorry I know. Just I am trying to maybe reassure myself that you guys can maybe shed some light on this soon."

"Any witnesses, persons of interest?"

"Nope no one."

"Well the team should hopefully come up with something within the week. What are there like three crime scenes? They plan on investigating all the crime scenes so I am sure something will pop up."

"I hope so" Mason replies with now an optimistic tone.
"Hey Mason what is this on the ground to this victim."

Mason walks towards Tom and looks at the picture.

"That is two ribs he cuts or I mean breaks out of some of the victims."

Mitchell leans over and looks too .He then reaches for another picture. He scours the picture and grabs another.

"There are no ribs missing on these two victims."

"Yeah that is the strange part. Those are the first two victims. No ribs were cut out. Then the next two he cut them out and laid them on the floor."

"What about the guy last night?"

"I am not sure I will find out when the evidence is brought in which should be sometime soon."

Mitchell sits back in the chair and studies the pictures.

"Why is it the first two victims were relatively unbloodied but then the next two were quite gory?"

"I believe something happened and he was angry. The killings were almost in like an enraged state and then he cuts out the ribs. "

"Well we should get to the scenes and then come back after the teams finish for the day."

"Good idea Tom. What kind of tool cut the bones?"

"We are not sure."

"What do you think the meaning of the ribs being pulled out?" Mason asks hoping maybe they had an answer.

"Not sure Mason. I need sometime to see what is going on. I need to see if this is a cult thing or something completely in other direction." Agent Mitchell glimpses opens up his laptop he transfers some of the data to a memory stick and then transfers it to his computer. He decides he will look some of it over at the hotel tonight and get an early jump start before they arrive at the first scene tomorrow.

"What was the time frame from the first pair to these?"

"About a couple of months."

"From them to last night?"

"Almost a week."

"Well either this guy got pissed off or…"

"Or what?" asks Mason reluctantly.

"He is bored and now he needs to satisfy he desire to kill by increasing the frequency and how he kills them. Creativity is the sign of a person with time on their hands and possibly a sign of boredom."

"That is not what we need to hear." says Mason as he puts his jacket on. It is 1115.

"Neither does the public." With that Mitchell looks up at Tom and Mason. Nothing is said. He packs his briefcase then they all grab their jackets and head out the door to the first crime scene.

The next day the agents get on the road at about 730. Not getting much sleep because of all the information Tom and Mitchell digested the previous they stop by the Wawa and grab a coffee. While pouring the coffee Tom hears some of the people inside talking about the FBI that were brought in. Curious to see what the overall feel was he takes his time pouring his vanilla nut bean coffee.

One of the husky construction guys not standing too far off is overheard.

"Yeah I heard thy brought in the crack unit of the FBI. Probably the police here are clueless and it got out." He says it to the girl behind the counter setting up the coffee bar.

"No I think when you get to a certain number of killings the government has to get involved. Like a quota or something." She says wiping the counter from the spilt coffee from the morning rush.

"Maybe they could just call in Scully and Mulder and get this resolved in an hour." The husky man says with a deep laugh. He is referring to the television show the Xfiles whom the two agents were sent in for the extraordinary cases which was an hour long show.

"Yes as long as we are not being bred to host aliens", she says laughing.

Tom looks around and notices the people around who are eavesdropping. Trying to get the newest information on the town's new but unwanted fame. Funny he thinks to himself would they be like this knowing he was an FBI agent or would they chase him like the paparazzi would to a movie star to get the newest scoop or picture. He knows soon he will find out once they start showing up on the daily updates on the television.

He stands in line and Mitchell falls right in behind him and they can hear the words of the arrival of the agents and they turn to each other and give each other a look like "he will go."

As Tom gets to the counter to pay he offers to pay for Mitchell's coffee and donut. Mitchell then grabs the local paper nearby and buys that too. He figures he can see how the local press handles the situation. If he needs to use them to get a message out he wants to familiarize himself with them.

It is 630 pm, the agents and Mason arrive back at the station. They visited the first two crime scenes .The agents didn't come up with a whole lot more information then what local authorities came up with. They await news from the lab and Quantico for hopefully some good information. They missed the CSI team at the first scene where nothing more was found. It was thoroughly clean. There no sign of a struggle so it is being assumed they were unconscious or even drugged throughout the ordeal. Everything that was found was stuff from the site not much was found that could have been said from somewhere else.

They packed up there around 3 or so and headed to the second scene.

Like the first scene they do a thorough sweep of the property. They went from house to house to try to see if anyone could remember anything from a few months back .They received a couple of clues but nothing that seemed to be a case breaker. Actually what they found was exactly what was expected –fear. People were answering there doors without even opening them. Talking through the doors seemed to be the norm. Even with police cars on the street that was not enough for some. Then there were those who were more then happy to talk to the police. Almost trying to be agents they would try to interject themselves into the crime by asking the cops what was going on and drawing up their own list of suspects or scenarios. All this is a result of fear.

Mason was thinking about how the town was dealing with this so differently form neighborhood to neighborhood. Like a virus everyone's reaction to the murders is different. Just like a virus those who still lived their lives normally amidst the murders were slowly infected with the fear that the other people were spreading. It is running rampant through this neighborhood and he hopes that it stays in the neighborhoods of the crime. Doubtful.

Even thought the crime labs from the feds were there they had not been able to say they found anything for sure. Mason can't tell from the Agent Mitchell and Tom's body language or conversation that they are onto something.

The talk in the vehicle's during the travel between the crime scenes is all about keeping in touch with the labs. Mason basically keeps quiet and answers any questions put to him.

They get back and decide they will wait for the results tomorrow and see if they can build anything from it.

"Well Mason tomorrow we would like to visit the third and fourth crime scenes if that is ok." Mitchell asks as he takes his coat off and sets his desk up to look over the information he gathered from during the day.

"Yes that should be no problem. I have my team going to be there in the early am to assist your men already."

"Great. I will go with you and Agent Crith is going to keep in touch with headquarters and see what he can come with on the inside. Also I have a note here saying that one of my teams did get into the third crime scene and they came up with a notebook left there which to them seemed out of place for some reason. They sent it to the local FBI agency to see what they can pull off of it. Maybe it was one of the victim's or maybe one of the local police here let but regardless we have it."

"Hmmn," Masons grunts." Not that I am aware of. I don't know any of our detectives who use notebooks anymore with all the technology that is being used it does seem a little antiquated even for our police force." Mason gives a light hearted laugh to loosen up the mood.

"Yeah true it is probably nothing anyways. So tell me anything good to get delivered here to eat tonight?"

"You guys want to eat here or go somewhere?" Mason looks at the clock and realizes it is running up on seven o clock.

'We prefer to eat here tonight .With it being our first night here we have a lot of catching up to do with the murders and need to spend time here reviewing." Agent Crith answers.

"Yeah probably tomorrow or the next day we will be able to go somewhere once we have some type of grip on this." Agent Mitchell adds.

"Well tell me what you are hungry for and I will go get it. Then I can come back and help you guys out."

"What do you think Tom, just pizza tonight?"

"Sounds good Mitch keep it simple. Just get us a pizza with extra cheese and pepperoni. Maybe a two liter of Coke with that too" Tom sits down at the table and opens his laptop up.

"Ok I will be back in about twenty minutes. After that I can stay as long as you need me." Mason feels energetic. He is excited he has fresh blood helping him now and he believes in these guys.

"Well Mason, we actually don't need any help tonight. Most of our work will be reading our notes along with other detective's notes. If I were you I jump on the chance to get home at a half decent hour and still have the murders being worked by us." Agent Mitchell responds.

Noticing Mason now seems puzzled or even possibly offended Agent Crith adds,"Yes Mason trust us, tomorrow you may not get the chance to go home this early."

Mason is a little hurt that he is not being involved in the investigation." Huh? Well ok if that works best for you guys .Well let me head off. I will call it in on my way out."

"Need money, here" Agent Mitchell reaches into his pocket and pulls out his wallet.

Mason puts his hand in the air to tell him to stop." No need tonight I have this. It is the least I could do. I am sure you will be here plenty of nights where you can pick up an order." He laughs and heads out the door.

The agents watch him through the window get into his car and pull out.

"You think he is pissed?"

"I don't think so Tom .He maybe offended like we don't trust him like he doesn't know how to handle the show. Deep down inside I bet a part of him is relieve and hoping we can come up with something that can put an end to this."

"I bet you are right. Riding around with him I have an impression he is a good and thorough detective. I just hope he doesn't lose his desire because he thinks we are taking the case from him." Agent Mitchell states as he looks over a couple of pictures he took at one of the scenes.

"Yeah. Anyways I didn't notice a lot of anything to build anything from .You?"

"Honestly, no. Part of me is worried. The crime scenes are too clean. This killer is extremely organized and careful. He has everything planned out all he way to the cleanup. He must prep for weeks in advance."

"Mean he could know his victims." Tom states.

"Or he doesn't and watches them, stalks them to where he knows every move they make .He knows their schedules .He knows when to attack and what is most efficient for him. Then when we go to the scenes tomorrow it seems he goes in another direction maybe it is here he makes his mistake. Maybe the rage involved has him lose his edge and he doesn't pay attention to everything he is doing."

"Yeah and whatever made him lose his edge happened in one week. What if he lost his edge because something personal was involved these victims? "

"Maybe it wasn't personal maybe something happened that he didn't account for that made him angry?" Mitchell throws out as he is starting to brainstorm.

"Or maybe one of the victims fought back hurt him and he went nuts?"

"Hey at this point no answer can be far fetched. Hopefully tomorrow we can piece some stuff together."

"You know what I really didn't see anything in common with these victims. Both from about the same social class. No criminal records. Not drug related. I am not sure what the emmo is about this guy .If we can figure out the common thing then we have something to start with."

Agent Mitchell starts to look some at some of the clues and tries to create something out of it. Just not enough evidence he thinks. He goes through his laptop which has some profiles stored from previous murderers. He overlooks a couple that he thinks has some similarities that maybe can help him see something he didn't see before. Damn it he thinks to himself why hasn't anything popped up yet. Mitchell is a persistent and hard working. Everything he does seem to always come together. He is one of the best profilers the FBI has to offer. He graduated first in his class. Considered by his professors to be one of the best students they have ever taught.

Almost in every aspect of his schooling Mitchell had excelled. From the physical regime he was one of toughest guys. Never has been really challenged almost by anyone in his class. Most of his classmates went to him for the answers. Even when Mitchell didn't have the answers he had the knack for finding ways to come up with answers.

He and Tom were roommates. Somewhat like night and day their interests were quite different but that is what made them good friends and great profilers. Since graduation Mitchell was instantly placed into the upper echelon of the FBI for criminal profiling. Granted it was a tough transition for there was some resentment from the veteran profilers who had to work there way up to the top of the class. After about a few months Mitchell seemed to have won them over with the same charisma and work ethic that worked for him in school.

His director took notice of his efforts. When another position was added to the department for the profilers due to the increase in serial murderers, rapists and other serious offenders he approached Mitchell and asked him about his old roommate Tom .Mitchell is puzzled why he is getting preferential treatment. Director Haskin explains to him he feels Mitchell would serve the agency better if he worked out in the field with the local authorities .He also explained he likes pairing up agents for various reasons.

He was going to pair him up with one of the agents from that office but did some investigating and researched Mitchell's background. He found that when paired with Todd their crime solved ratio was incredible and decided to bring Tom to the department and have him with Mitchell out in the field but wanted to make sure that nothing had changed between them and did not want to bring onboard without talking to Mitchell about it. When he introduced the idea to Mitchell, Mitchell was excited about it but did ask if it would have had a ripple effect in the office. He was also concerned if the progress he made with the unit would take a step back with what looked like preferential treatment. Director Haskin explained to him he threw the idea out to the group first and no one was against it.

Mainly because everyone understood Mitchell's work in the office was now limited since there is so much field work to do. Upon hearing this Mitchell did not need to give it much thought and almost instantly agreed to the idea.

Within a month Tom was brought aboard. After about a month of learning protocol Mitchell and Tom were sent out to a serial rapist case in North Carolina. The case had them there for 2 weeks which a surprise to everyone since a previous pair of agents was involved for over three months could not crack the case. They found angles in the case that no one was able to come upon.

They have worked together for over 4 years and have developed a reputation of being a tenacious pair that together has no flaws. Tom is detail oriented and has some street smarts that balances out the pair where Mitchell is book smarter.

Overall they have solved a couple of the most complexed and notorious crimes in the country. The Smiley Face Killer was the most prolific crime they had worked on. It was the longest running case before they got involved and the longest one for them to have cracked. It was that case that almost broke Mitchell as an agent. The gore and sadistic images bothered Mitchell like no other had done before. He never encountered crimes so heinous that he would have trouble sleeping eventually it started to affect his work then carried over to his personality. After noticing a change going on internally in Mitchell Tom called Haskin and requested maybe someone come down and talk to Mitchell.

Haskin sent down a psychologist who talked to Mitchell and helped him out. Mitchell took a two week leave where he left to go back home and clear his head. Afterwards Mitchell came back to the case where he never had issues again with the case. Tom head his ground good and developed a stronger opinion of himself from his peers. He actually figured the armed forces angle and when Mitchell came back they were together on it and eventually would crack the case. When they returned to Quantico they were praised for their work.

Since that case nothing has compared as in length or the absolute horror they encountered.

On their way up to this case after reading the case Mitchell somewhat was optimistic this wouldn't be so bad. Right now though as he looks over the notes he must prepare himself for a slightly longer stay then they thought.

His attention is broken up by a set of headlights glaring in the window.

"Ahhh food. God am I hungry." Tom says as he closes a folder of pictures and heads to a table in the room and clears it off so he can eat.

Mason walks in and asks" Ok you guys hungry?"

"Absolutely. Wow it seemed like that was a lot quicker then I thought." Mitchell states looking at him heading towards the table.

"They weren't busy so I guess it was easy to prepare. "He sets down the food."You guys need anything else?"

Tom and Mitchell look at each other."No I think we are fine." answers Mitchell.

"Well if you guys don't mind I am going to head out. I will be in early tomorrow .Is that fine?"

"Sounds great. We will probably be here for a couple of hours and then head off and see you tomorrow. Should we meet at the crime scene or here?"

"Whatever you prefer." Mason answers not really caring.

"How about we meet there that way we don't get tied up with the media or anything else going on here. We have the address and we will be there about 8?" asks Tom.

"Sounds good 8 it is." With that Mason waves good bye and heads out the door to his vehicle.

"Well dig in. I don't think we will be here a lot longer tonight. I have a feeling tomorrow will be the day we really get a feel for what is going on." Mitchell says.

"I think you are right. " Tom reaches for a napkin and wipes the sauce dripping off his face. "Damn maybe it might not be that bad if we are here for a little bit." He says with a laugh.

"You remember you said that in a month or two. OK?" Mitchell replies back laughing with his mouth half full.

After 15 minutes of eating they get back to work for about another hour and a half. Then they head to the local hotel to get some sleep they have a long day ahead of them.

Feeling an elbow in his side Mason rolls over with half a grunt and asks what she wants.

"The alarm went off .Didn't you hear it?"

Mason rubs his eyes and looks towards the clock and replies,"No, how long ago you set it for?"

"I set it for 700 because you said last night you were going to meet them at the scene and could get up a little later." She tells him as she moves closer. He looks at her and appreciates how supportive she is. With all that is going on he didn't even remember to make sure the alarm clock was set last night. Funny regardless however he never misses when the clock goes off he is pretty much on top of it. Since he was able to leave at almost a normal time from the office like before all the murders happened he forgot for at least one night about going to bed late. He went to bed after her but a couple before what has lately has been the norm. He was been slightly more irritable but he didn't think it was from just the case but the lack of sleep from the images the case has given him. He was thinking about going to see a therapist to help him through this mentally and medically so he can get back into a somewhat normal sleeping pattern. Last night was the first almost normal night he has had in weeks.

"Ok thanks Hun. Oh God."

"What is wrong?" she asks as she lies in his arms.

"Oh nothing just hoping today gives us the littlest hint of something positive. I just realized since they have been here there has been not a lot to cheer about. I know I am impatient so I hope that something pops up."

"Well how about before you go beating yourself silly why don't you wait and see what they came up with from last night or wait to see what happens today." She tries he best impression of a person who is confident and strong for him.

"You are the best even though your acting stinks." He laughs and gives her a kiss on her forehead and gets out of bed.

"I am going to get a shower then I will be out of here in about a half hour so if you need anything let me know." With that he grabs the towel of the back of his chair and turns the shower.

"Do you want to me to make you breakfast?"

He pokes his head out the door and thinks for a second," You know what? Just toast me a bagel with cream cheese. Is that ok?"

"No problem." She heads down the steps to the kitchen and to prepare his breakfast.

Within about twenty minutes Mason comes down the steps and walks up to her grabs her from behind and kisses her.

"Thanks for making me breakfast. By the way anything special tonight for dinner? "

"I haven't thought about it why?"

"Well maybe we can go to the Chinese joint for dinner."

"That doesn't sound like a bad idea actually but when will you be home?" she turns around and sets a plate up for her breakfast.

"Well unless there is some big break I am going to assume like 6-7 or so. Who knows if it is like yesterday's results look at the earlier side."

"You know whatever happens I can wait and if it is late well I am sure I can miss a meal or grab a snack to hold me over."

Mason eats his bagel and briefly looks at the newspaper. Well at last there was not another murder last night he thinks by looking at the headline. He folds the paper and flips through the channels. He comes to ESPN news and catches up on the injury updates for his fantasy league. He gets up puts his plate in the sink and looks at the clock it is 745 and he starts to leave.

"Hey don't forget my family is coming over tomorrow." Melissa says as she grabs a napkin.

Looking up at her he tilts his head and asks why.

"Because my sister and her family are in town. We decided everyone would get together tomorrow night since they leave the following day to head back home. We are having turkey and all the fixings."

"Oh yeah I remember that now. Almost like having a second Thanksgiving. I will definitely be looking forward to dinner tomorrow."

"Well I am going I am probably already late .You know those feds play everything to the book."He gives her a kiss and advances towards the front door.

"Well listen if you run real late just give me a heads up and I will make myself dinner here. No big deal if that happens." She hopes in a way they do have dinner maybe he will start to become himself again.

"I will, love you." Mason says as he closes the door heading out.

"Love you too." Good luck she says to herself. She stands out the window and waves him .She wonders how strong will this make him or how it will break him. She turns around and tends to the house; she can't bear thinking about the misery he has been going through.

Mason jumps into his car and starts pulling out of his driveway and stops. He looks into his rear view to make sure he didn't miss any spots from breakfast on his face. He turns on the radio and tries to forget about the crisis in the town. He has flipped through a few stations and not one is talking about a murder. Ahh almost like it use to be. Last night was a quiet night and they can use quite a few more nights like that.

He heads towards the latest crime scene and decides to call Mitch and see if they are already there.

"Agent Mitchell here."

"Hey Mitchell it is Mason. I was calling to see if you are already there?"

"We are about ten minutes away. We are meeting up with a forensics team with some equipment that was overnighted here. We are hoping this equipment helps shed a light on what is going on. The team yesterday struck out trying to come up with some new evidence and we guess they ordered the high tech toys." Mitchell tries to deliver the news in a nonchalant way not giving Mason any doubts so early in the government's arrival.

"Well I guess I shouldn't feel too bad if you guys aren't coming up with anything." Mason actually feels a little bit better. If they would have come up with a lot of evidence it may have had a negative effect on the department, internally and with the public.

"I told you I was confident you and your men did your job thoroughly. I was sort of hoping that they came up with at least one piece of evidence that wasn't uncovered."

"Well me too. Anything that can help bring this case closer to being solved I won't complain about." Mason says with a chuckle it has been awhile since he has cracked a joke when he was on the job. He does feel a little bit relieved now that he has qualified help .At first he did feel uncomfortable but having a night to sleep on it he consciously knew it was needed and best for everyone.

"Ok well I will see you in about five minutes. Do you guys need anything?" Mason asks knowing he was stopping at the Wawa for a coffee.

Agent Mitchell looks over to agent Crith and asks if he needs anything . They both needs agree on cappuccinos.

The Wawa will throw Mason about five more minutes out of his way but that is the least he can do for these guys especially of they end up they close this case quicker then his force would have.

In a few minutes he pulls up to the Wawa and gets out. A few locals look at him and greet him with a smile. Mason can see the smiles are false faces. These people are scared but they do their best to live their lives like nothing is wrong. Mason heads to the cappuccino bar and grabs everyone what they requested and grabs a dozen of donuts while he is at it.

Ten minutes he is at the third crime scene and catches up with the agents. They all stand outside and drink their coffees. They split the donuts among the themselves .They mention to one of the team members donuts were available... When they are done the clean their hands and are greeted by the forensics team that has been there since 630 am.

"How are you? I am Dr Driker. I am head of this unit." The gentleman is tall in stature and has a commanding appearance to himself. He is about six foot three, 45 years old, brown receding hair line and a pale complexion.

Mason introduces himself to the doctor and then Mitchell starts the conversation.

"Well any luck so far?" Mitchell says hoping that something good is about to be stated.

"No nothing. Either your men cleaned this place up extremely well or your killer is very meticulous."

"Well it seems to be the latter of the two unfortunately here." Mason answers.

"Is it ok we come in John?" Mitchell asks. Obviously knowing this doctor probably from previous cases.

"Sure there really is nothing you can mess up. There is no spot we have quarantined off. The murders happened downstairs .The blood is dry and doesn't seem like anyone has been through to do any clean up."

"No they were specifically told, the victims relatives that is, not to clean or touch anything in the house. They actually had no problem. They had no want to go in and deal with the situation."

"Well that is good then we know exactly what the killer is doing or not doing in these situations." Dr Driker answers." Also Mitchell we took a couple more blood samples to make sure there isn't a third one that maybe the killer in case of a struggle or accident on his part."

"Hey whatever works. You're the doctor. Well we are going in probably down in the basement to start."

"Go ahead my team is on the first and second floors. When we are done here we are going to head to the next crime scene and if it is like the first three I have a feeling we will be out of there by 2 o clock." Dr Driker responds while looking over the neighborhood.

"Hey John, help yourself to the donuts. I think there is enough for your team. "

"I will actually. I was running behind at the hotel this morning and didn't grab breakfast. Thanks. "He rummages through the box looking at what remained.

With that Mason and the agents head into the house slowly peeking around what was on the first floor as they advanced down towards the basement. Mason notices no struggle of any type on the first floor.

"Thinking the same thing as me?" Agent Crith asks Mason.

"No struggle?"

"Yep."

They start heading down the stairs where a damp wet smell has a pungent scent along with it. It is the smell of death. It is a thick smell that at first chokes Mason who needs to adjust. He doesn't recall it being that bad the night of the crime. Mason looks around a chair is on its side where the male victim was found laying. He looks across the room where the other chair is sitting upright where he found the female victim. It is soaked in blood as if someone poured paint over the chair and just let it rundown the chair .Thick in some areas where it looks like three coats of paint were applied. The scene still is unbearable. Imagining what they went through is beyond belief. No one should be subject to this fate-no one. Mason looks over at the agents to see their reaction to the scene now that they are actually there. Mitchell is in deep trance probably picturing the murder through his head while Todd is over in the corner looking on the ground for any clues.

"What do you think he drugged them downstairs? I think maybe he had a gun or something I can't see how two people are forced downstairs with no resistance? Doesn't make sense and on top of that they don't both live here."

"Yes we thought that was strange too. We asked family members for both victims if the two knew each other and the answers were no. We think he somehow was invited in. Then he made his move and forced her downstairs where he ties her up. Afterwards he goes back outside to his vehicle and brings the victim down and the ties him up." Mason says as the men head down the steps.

"She justs stays there and he is comfortable that she won't escape as he is getting the other victim? Is the other victim already dead though?" Mitchell asks as he bends over observing the chair the woman was strapped to.

"Yes he ties in her so good she can't escape. The time of death was determined to be minutes apart for both victims."

"We could not find any drugs in either person's system on first tests. I think the guy was knocked out then killed first. There was actual evidence of his blood dry on the wall and since the basement is damp we came to the conclusion he was killed first because none of the blood from the female had dried."

Agent Crith takes pictures from various spots in the basement.

"How was it made known there was a murder here Mason?" He asks while snapping pictures.

"The neighbor noticed the door open and being cold outside and her living alone something didn't seem right. He says he came to the door and called for her but no response. So when that happened he knew he should get the police involved. It was 1140 pm."

"So the murders happened somewhere between when it got dark, which is about what here? 630 or so?"

"Sort of there more like 6 to 630."Mason responds.

"So from 630 to about 1130 these murders took place."

Right then the voice of Dr. Driker intervenes into the conversation.

"If the basement was as damp as it is now the blood to have dried like in the pictures I saw would have had to happen in like a 2 hour window at the max. Then makes the crime occur around 930 pm which is plenty dark to bring a body inside. Being a work night and school night no surprise no one knows anything."

"Very true. You think our murderer plans it like this with it down to a science or is it just irony?" asks Dr. Driker to the group.

"I hope it is irony because he thinks it out this much we may have ourselves a problem men." Mitchell states as he heads back to the steps.

"You know there is nothing more here then what I saw in the pictures. This is like yesterday. Only difference is the violence carried out in the murders is different. I am going to look around the other floors to see if he ventured there maybe we can try to find a link between the two victims or maybe even the other crime scenes." Mitchell heads up while agent Crith heads into a different section of the basement for more pictures. Mason justs stands there and remembers what it was like the night of the murder. How the force was pale faced from the gore and complexity of the murders. Now he sees a confident team of forensics that has shown veteran leadership with dealing with these kind of issues.

"Hey Todd, I am going to head up to incase you go looking for me."

"No problem I should only be down here like another minute or so."

Mason heads up and hears Mitchell upstairs on the second floor. He again walks around and sees nothing out of the norm just like the original night he was out there.

The agents spend about a half hour more there and decide to head to the next scene. They and the team bring out a couple bags of evidence that they hope will help them in some way.

They head to the next scene where a hour into the investigation Mason gets called back into the office to interview a couple of possible witnesses. Those have been scarce in this case and he jumps right on it leaving the agents to themselves to come up with something. There are two CSI units there on this one. The first CSI unit has caught up to the second one trying to figure what happened to this one.

In the living is a white room that is painted red in blood.

"Hey Mitch I saw the pictures for this one but they were when the victim was removed. I didn't see the ones of him murdered. What happened? I mean my God what is going on here? There is more blood here then the first scene and that one was extremely gory." Mason sort of swallows hard knowing he doesn't want to really know what happened but knows he needs to. This was the case he was not called into and the feds came right in so Mason is not informed at all about this case.

"What we found was the victim laying on the ground face up but chest down." Starts Mitchell.

"What?" Mason asks puzzled.

"The torso was facing downwards but the head was almost twisted off to where it was facing upwards. We believe his head was almost twisted without an incision .In other words when the skin could not stretch anymore it just tore and the blood splattered everywhere. " Mason looks over at a wall where there is a hand print from blood.

"How the hell could he move if his head was almost ripped off?" asks Mason referring to the handprint coming after the head being twisted.

"The head was not twisted before that. There was more torture before the head twisting which is what killed him. He had his ankles both sliced behind the heel where the Achilles is. We think he grabbed his ankles and that is where the blood on the wall came from." Mitchell fills in Mason as Todd then joins the conversation.

"He basically immobilized the victim and then was stood above him and killed him."

"How the hell could he have done that? I mean the force to just break the neck is tough but the elasticity in the skin should have given him enough trouble. Are talking a guy with incredible strength or am I just clueless to what is involved here?"

"Yes we believe the strength scenario but we also think he was assisted with a tool or vice or something." answers Mitchell.

"Where was the point of entrance?"

"We think the killer was already inside and when the victim got home he attacked him when he was sitting on the couch. "No struggle again and we think somehow he sliced the ankles while the victim was the couch." Todd heads to the couch where he points to two separate streaks of blood running away from the couch." Possibly facing face down and the killer struck that way which prevented the victim from getting up and fighting him or running."

"All the damage or any disturbances were here in the living room. The rest of the house is in normal shape." Todd states.

"My God what has happened .Something had to trip this guy out to make him go and kill in a ravaged way .This is not how it started." Mason is trying to comprehend and make sense of the changes in the murders.

"It was probably best you didn't come that night we think it was a worse scene then the other two murders."

Mason walks around the living room and looks for any clues.

"No pictures. He lives alone? Family?"

"No Mason the man lives alone and no family. He was a public figure we believe someone said that night."

"Oh really? What was his name? "

Todd looks at Mitchell with a puzzled look." I am not sure .Do you have the paperwork or remember?" he asks Mitchell .

"No paperwork it is out in the car. I thought his name was like some time of nickname or something. Champ .Ace. Hell I don't remember."

"Ahh don't worry about it not a big deal. I will look it up at the office later." responds Mason. He then gets a phone call on his cell and it is the station.

"Excuse me guys." Mason walks away and answers the phone."

"Mason here."

Mitchell and Todd go back into collecting notes or evidence that may help them out. A few minutes later Mason walks back in.

"Hey guys I am going to have to roll out. That was the station and get this two people just came in and are giving information they think that may have at two of the murders."

"Is it credible? What did they say?" Mitchell asks a little excitement in his voice.

"No more information was given. They want me to come there and interview them. I will call you guys if this crime scene is relevant to either of the witnesses. Otherwise I will get my men out to the scenes and see if they can come up with something we can follow up on."

"Ok sounds good. If we come up with anything we will keep you updated."

"Great I'll have my cell phone on me if you need me." Mason then takes one more look at the crime scene where he then walks out the front door and heads to his vehicle.

He drives back to the station and on his way back he calls his wife and they talk briefly he updates her with really no news but he enjoys talking to her at least once a day. It is refreshing to him. When the day drags or he gets boggled up nothing puts him to ease like the sound of her voice.

After the conversation he pulls up to the station and interviews two people who had information about two different scenes. One witness stated they saw a van leaving the area where the two people were killed in the basement of the house. Mason forwarded the information to a couple of officers who went to the area and asked questions. What they came up with was an electrician was doing work late that night a few houses down.

The second witness stated hearing like a tractor trailer driving through the neighborhood one night during the second murder. When asked why she waited so long to report it her answer was she heard it again last night and it was the same sound and no trailers are permitted on her street so the sound really stands out.

Mason again forwarded the information to another officer whom after doing some research in the area found it was a furniture delivery truck. When he called the company they went back in their records to confirm a delivery was made in that neighborhood earlier that night of the murder. Two witnesses, two murders, two dead ends. Mason knew it was too good to be true.

It is about lunchtime and Mason decides to head home for lunch .He calls Mitchell to find out they are still on site looking around and will grab lunch after they are done which should be about an hour.

He arrives home about 130 and sits down. His wife had lunch prepared already for him. They discuss the day so far then she reminds him to try to be home on time for her family and help cook some of the dinner. She already has the turkey in the oven at the same time she is working the stuffing and potatoes.

Within about an hour Mason gets up and heads back to the station. No phone calls from anyone can only have him assume there were no breaks found.

He gets back to the station in about ten minutes where he finds out the agents should be there in fifteen minutes but they did not find anything.

He sits in the lunchroom and waits for them. While waiting watches the daily press conferences that go on outside on the television. Same old same old he thinks. Why even waste anyone's time telling them you have no clue about this psycho and you just have to wait till he kills again. God damn that is so reassuring he thinks.

Then the agents pull up to the station where they are swarmed by the media but you can tell they found nothing. Within a minute the media walks away with their heads dangling looking at the ground looking like beaten dogs, there is nothing new to report.

They walk and have a meeting in the conference room which lasts about an hour discussing what they found or didn't find plus any scenarios or thoughts of what is going on. Agent Mitchell though tells them he can not come up with a profile there is not enough evidence nor does these murders follow any other pattern they have encounter but he says something will break they just need patience.

By this time it is about 430 and Mason mentions he will be cutting out on time the next day due to his family coming over for a big dinner. No one has any complaints. He sits at his desk and reviews what he had done today. He gets so mesmerized by the case he doesn't realize it is almost 540 and he starts putting the files and evidence together. He remembers he was to go out for dinner. He pushes away from his desk and heads towards the agents in the other office to see if they have found anything and mention he will be cutting out.

"Find anything Mitch? "

"Not really. Still trying to find similarities in the case and will have found nothing. We can find things in common for a pair or three but then the one or two other victims did not fit in at all so we have to start with a new starting point and see where it takes us." Todd answers for Mitchell who seems in thought about a document he is looking at.

"Well what did you find?"

"We have found the two victims killed in the first house we were out earlier both drove BMWs. Both had good income. We checked where they purchased the cars and two different dealerships. Then…" Mason interrupts him.

"The other two I thought had good paying jobs. They didn't have maybe a BMW in the garage that was the spouse's?"

"Nope one was a Cherokee and the other was a Honda Accord. "

"Maybe it is the social classes maybe the killer doesn't like wealthy people?"

Mitchell now interjects himself into the conversation.

"No the one victim only made about $26000 while two of them were over $100000. We tried churches, gyms social clubs, bars, anything that would draw these people together but nothing that sticks them all together. There is just something strange about all these cases. We seem we can't profile this guy even after a few days of looking over the scenes and evidence."

"Well that is not exactly what I wanted to hear." replies Mason.

"Yeh but trust me something will fall into spot .How about you?"

"Nothing. I figured I would come back here see if you found anything because I am heading out. I had a roller coaster of a day from the crimes scene to thinking we had a couple of witnesses to find out they added nothing to the investigation. I will be back at it tomorrow, early in the morning. I have her family coming for a dinner almost like a Thanksgiving meal. Tomorrow night so I am going to have an early start so I can leave at a decent time."

"Special occasion?" asks Todd as he leans back into his chair listening.

"No just her sister came by from out of state and they decided to take advantage of the chance and get everyone together since they leave the next day."

"That's cool to have a family like that. Mine is somewhat like that. My parents always have the relatives over on the holidays or take advantage of the nice weather and jump on it by inviting them over in the summer ." answers Mitchell.

Todd chimes in." So what leftovers should I expect to see on Thursday? Or should I ask what are you bringing me?"

"Hey over there! What is this me thing? Try us partner." Mitchell blurts out with a laugh.

"Well my wife makes a mean stuffing and I will be sure to bring in a slice of her sister's cherry cheesecake."

"Not a slice my man try slices, I am not sharing with you guys." Todd breaks out in a laugh.

"Ok ok I will see what I can scarf up and I will bring it in. Geez dinner is hasn't even happened yet and I am already taking orders."

"Hey Mason we'll call you if anything pops up as in a break in the case."

"I won't be holding my breath." Mason says not trying to kill the mood of the room which seemed like these guys worked together for a lot longer then a few days.

"Yeah we know. Have a good night." Mason waves good bye to the agents and heads out the door it is 555 and he thinks he should be home by 615.

He heads out to the car and realizes these guys were nothing like he anticipated. They would fit in with his guys with no problems. They have a good cohesiveness.

He jumps in his car and looks forward to a nice time with his wife.

It is Thursday and about 445. Mason who was driving through a couple of the neighborhoods doing follow up interviews. His day is over so now he heads home to get ready and prepare for the big dinner.

He pulls up in the driveway and sees the car of her sister is already there. He grabs his laptop case and heads in.

"Hey Honey. "He greets his wife at the counter and gives her a kiss on the cheek. "Hey Vicky long time no see. How are you?"

"I am great Mason. I hear you have your hands full. I pray for you every night that things will work out for you."

"Thanks Vicky. How is the family?"

"They are in the other room. Everyone is getting big."

"Let me go see for myself." Mason heads into the living room where Vicky's husband Bill and their son Bill Jr are playing."

Mason greets them and spends a few minutes talking to them.

In the kitchen Jill and her sister talk about Mason's welfare. Jill tells her he has his weak moments.

About twenty minutes later the rest of the family shows up and sits down for dinner. It is a pleasant scene and Mason absorbs the moment. All the chaos and rhetoric seems so far away. He sees smiles of the people he loves and knows. The murders seem to be an afterthought at this moment.

For the next hour they sit, eat, and tell jokes and stories. There is reflection of what has brought them there that day.

After dinner the ladies start cleaning up the table and they guys go into the den and watch television. In a little bit Mason gets up and heads into the kitchen. When he gets there he heads to the little island and starts cleaning off the turkey. He grabs a Tupperware container and starts peeling the turkey clean.

Little William walks in and asks his uncle a question.

"Hey Uncle Mason."

"Yes William."

"Did you grab the wishbone yet? I want to go against my dad."

"Sure one second here."

Mason finds it and as he pulls it he stops He stares at it deeply like it making some telepathic connection to him. His face goes from happy to fearful. His eyes remain fixed on the turkey and the wishbone.

"Oh my God .That is what it means." He blurts out as the family watches he reacts like he had just seen a ghost. He is thinking about the advice Marie told him the killer is wishing them luck. The ribs being ripped out are that to resemble a wishbone. All this time and now it comes to him. This is what she meant. He thinks how the hell did she know that but then he thinks about the situation at hand. He is going to call Mitchell and let him know. He looks at the clock and it is about 830.

"What are you talking about honey?" asks Melissa who saw the demeanor of her husband completely change.

"He is toying with us. He is wishing us luck." Mason hands William the bone and runs to grab his cell phone and heads outside. He calls up Mitchell and tells he knows what the two ribs are ripped out the body for. It is a symbol and a calling card wishing the authorities luck.

Just like snipers use an ace from a deck of cards as their calling card he is using the person's ribs.

Mitchell thinks about it for a few minutes and agrees. They now realize this is worse then they thought .The killer has no respect that they can figure out what is doing. He is taunting them.

They will meet tomorrow at 8 am and see if this revelation somehow can lead them somehow that they have overlooked.

He walks back into the house after he gets of the phone and finishes cleaning the turkey off. His wife doesn't want to bring anything up and change the mood that is quite warming in the house.

They all head into the living room where they decide to play a game of Pictionary. Mason plays but his mind is miles away but yet doesn't let it ruin the night for anyone. After about an hour of playing the group starts to break up and head to the kitchen for dessert. Mason cuts a piece of that infamous cheesecake for himself and adds some cool whip to the top.

He sits at the dining table where the conversation is anything but the obvious. He actually appreciates that no one is bringing up the murders. They all talk about the family summer picnic and when to have it.

At about 1130 or so everyone has left the house .Mason is tired and heads up to bed. He hopes that what he has figured out gives them a fresh starting point. He goes to the bathroom and brushes his teeth. Gets changed for bed and lays in it. He can hear Melissa almost done cleaning up. Melissa proceeds upstairs a few minutes later but he is already asleep.

She bends over and gives him a kiss on his cheek.

At about 8 pm that same night Lance decides to run to the grocery store for a few items for the next day for him and Jill. He walks through the door and sees Amy is working the self serve registers he smiles at her but she can't se him. He notices a black man about 6 foot standing over her looking like he is harassing her. He is wearing a bright orange parka with what looks like brand new orange boots. Lance sort of laughs to himself thinking he wouldn't be caught in what looks like a clown suit. He looks at Amy's body language and it seems to reflect exactly what he is thinking. He stops at the magazine rack where he came in and inconspicuously watches what is going on. He notices a few customers coming up to the registers and the big black guy backs off and walks away from the area. Giving it another minute the guy seems to get lost in to the store and Lance decides to continue what he wanted to do there.

About five to ten minutes goes by and he is done his shopping .He proceeds towards the registers Amy is working and again she has that same man over her almost hounding her. Lance can now hear the conversation and it seems like there is an argument. He looks at her and she acknowledges him with a faint smile. She seems embarrassed by the situation. Lance continues to unpack his groceries where he can hear the man is belittling her for working at the grocery store. Lance can't get the full account of what t is about and doesn't want to intervene unless he had all the information. He does look over again and sees she is distraught over the pestering but when Lance decides to suggest enough of the harassment the man leaves in a bit of a fit.

He is done checking his stuff out and bagging it .He then looks over at her.

"You ok over there?" he asks softly.

"Yes I am fine. Some people just can't take no for an answer. He is such an ass." Her voice sounds angry and bitter. Before Lance can say more another employee walks up and relieves Amy from the register for her break.

She says to him. "You in a rush?"

"Not really why do you want to talk?"

"Sure I don't want to be ignorant but I get a ten minute break and didn't want to blow you off. I want to go outside and eat my snack and drink."

"Fine with me .This way?"

"Yep." They both head out the doors and head about twenty more feet to a bench where they both sit down.

"So what was that all about?"he asks." Boyfriend? Or a guy that won't get a date with you?"

"Neither .It is a guy that wants me to run drugs for him and says I am wasting my time here and not going anywhere and he can deliver me from the hands of hell. What an asshole. I have a kid and I don't need to stupid shit like that nor would I if I didn't have a child." She is very angry at this man and obviously doesn't respect him.

"Drug dealer?" asks Lance.

"Yes like Mr. I dropped out of school in tenth grade and now I sell drugs eight years later. They call him Sky High"

"Why didn't you tell him to leave?"

"I did but he doesn't take no for an answer then he somewhat threaten me by saying if I make a scene then he will set me up and have me lose this job. He is crazy and I don't want him screwing my life up. If I have to deal with his shit for five minutes about once a month or so to be his little flygirl so be it. I will deal with it at last my kid is eating."

"He threatened you seriously?" asks Lance getting angry now.

"Yes he thinks because he supplies the town money drives a better car then the educated folk around here and has more money then them that he is the god damn king."

"This guy from around here? I don't think I have seen him before."

"Yeah he is from the west side. He hangs out Shiffer park alone that is where he makes his deals. He does it all him self so he can save money by not paying runners."

"Well why did he offer you a job if he has no one else doing it?"

"He wants to get in my pants and thinks this could be a way. He must think I am unhappy doing this and he would by my hero and in return I could repay him with sex."

"Good girl. You have your head on right see. Don't let a piece of shit like that bring you down. You do what you know best, work hard and be a great mom. He eventually will get caught. His happiness is short term yours is long term just remember that.'

"Oh I will Lance. I can't wait till he gets busted and he thinks all these people who look up to him will leave him hanging. Then we will see how cool and great he is." She finishes up her cookies and soda .She looks a little bit relieved by talking about it. After another minute she looks like she is ready to go back in.

"Well you better get in there your ten minutes is almost up."

She looks at her watch and agrees with him." Thanks for letting me vent Lance I appreciate it."

"Hey anytime you need a punching bag you look me up don't let anyone bring you down or intimidate you."

"Oh I know. Have a good one and see you soon." She waves to him as she heads into the store he waves back.

He gets to his car and puts the groceries in the trunk .He walks around to the driver's side and checks his watch he is going to be home a little later then expected. He has a trip to Shiffer Park he must make first.

Within the hour Lance drives by Shiffer Park and does not see the man they call Sky High. This was unexpected to him not planning on killing someone tonight. As he drove towards the park and as he was driving around he contemplated how he was to do this. Part of him doesn't want to be there. He always prepares when he is going to kill someone. He hasn't researched anything here. He knows he has the usual tools of his trade in his vehicle but still this is almost too impulsive.

He finally decides to do it. He will not leave the body out to be found though. It would be too suspicious especially if Amy would find out. He will take the body to the Hatsin Warehouse and throw it in the pit down in the basement that was an old sewer access back in the early sixties. Throw some garbage on top and he will never be found. He used this place before and made himself acquainted with its structure.

He makes a turn around a block and decides he will give it ten more minutes. He turns his lights off and just sits there. He has never staked out a drug dealer so he only assumes what he is looking for. After fiddling around with the radio to occupy his time he sees movement through the park about 30 yards away. There are lights in the park which has a basketball court that is lit. He looks around and sees trees that also cast a lot of shadows which he is sure to take advantage of. The person in the foreground seems to stop at what looks like a park bench. A light just does cast enough for him to make out an orange glow. This is his man.

He looks around to see if there is a spot closer to where Sky is sitting. He plans on attacking him at the bench only if he can move the car closer to drag him over there. He looks and does see a couple of spots closer that he could make and not have been made. He puts the car into drive and does not turn the lights on. He moves slowly through the park to where he wants to go, He pays attention to Sky to see if he is watching but it looks like Sky is turned away and possibly on the phone. It is about 915 and the park is empty and the area is barren. With the time of the year the only people out here he is sure are drug dealers or buyers. He parks his car and turns the engine off. He turns around and grabs a pipe from under the passenger seat that he put there for protection. He puts it next to him and thinks of the best path to get there .He is about thirty yards away and looks where he can sneak up. If Sky stays the way he is then he is in good shape.

He gets out of the car and plans on knocking the bastard out .He will kill him at the warehouse. He double checks to make sure he has the tie wraps in his pocket so he can tie up the arms and legs. As he approaches Sky he can hear that he is on the phone talking. Sticking to the shadows for cover he hops from one to the other paying strict attention to being silent. He is within fifteen feet and was waiting for Sky to get off the phone .He is standing behind a tall bush and takes a look around to make sure no one is around. After feeling he checked the area out he now just waits for the phone call to end. He can the conversation is about how much money he has made dealing for the day and about a party he plans on having in the next month.

Lance is sick thinking this bastard put down a person that works hard and wants to do it right. This isn't the typical person he would murder. Most of the time these victims had jobs of power and control the fabric of the people beneath them. This guy though has no job and this is different yet it is the same in the situation with Amy. A low life scum trying to make some miserable with threats and degrading her .He is making her feel inferior to himself, a piece of shit. That is where he can draw a common line with Sky and his previous victims. This in reality is no different. He grips the pipe tighter to where his knuckles turn into a glowing white from the pressure. He has the feeling the anger starting to bubble over inside himself like lava oozing itself over the top of a volcano.

Then it happens. Sky is heard saying good bye and tucks in phone back in his jacket and just sits there. Lance takes another look around and decides it is time. He slowly walks towards him paying attention not to step on any sticks or anything else that will give him away. He closes in ten feet then five to where he is in arms reach. He raises his arm and with one powerful stroke like he was about to beat a rug he let's go. Sky turns his head towards the swing and the pipe catches him on the rear jaw behind the ear. A sickening sound is made almost like that of a glow stick being snapped to turn on. Lance notices blood spill out form his mouth and towards the ground it splatters. Sky falls to the ground and hits it hard.

Lance knows he is knocked out by the way he hits the ground. The arms never extend to break the fall. Lance stands over him for a brief second and sees the blood coming out. He then pulls out a sock and shoves it in Sky's mouth to catch the blood so it doesn't create a trail. He wraps duct tape around the mouth then starts to drag the body towards the car. Sky is tall but not heavy so he doesn't seem hard to move. Within a minute he gets him to the back of the car and pops open the trunk where he has a little difficulty getting him in the car because of Sky's length. Once in he closes the trunk quietly, He pauses then listens and looks neither sounds nor movements from neither the trunk nor the area. He gets in the car, starts it and pulls away with the lights out till he is about two blocks away then he turns them on and heads to the warehouse.

He looks at the clock and realizes he can't make this a project. It is bad enough she has already left work and he didn't get to see her off but now he has to come up with an excuse where he was. He reaches for his cell phone and fiddles with the buttons thinking of what he is going to say that rerouted him over an hour and a half. Damn it he thinks. Why didn't he just let it be? Why did this one person who has a negative value on society throw him out of his cycle? The answer is because the dealer was a negative value just like the people who are portrayed as productive, positive influences in society. How can a person who ruins so many lives and can dictate how a person can feel or think be positive? They aren't. Lance has determined that and can't be persuaded otherwise.

Ok. He decides to say he has been rerouted by a friend and was convinced to go and grab a bite with him. They discussed the personal issues his friend has. He can make it work with her since she knows he is a caring person and a great friend to whomever is in need.

He calls her up and finds out she is approaching her work. She does ask him what happened to him and he responds with his original story saying he went out with a buddy and they grabbed a few drinks. He tells her he went back to buddy's house and sat around. She was fine with that as long as she sees him in the morning. He promises there will be no reason not to. He tells her he loves her and they will chat tomorrow. He hangs up and focuses on the matter at hand.

He is about a few minutes away. He is going to the Hatsin warehouse where he will kill and dispose of the body. There is a well in the basement in what now is a secret room. The well was more like an oversize drain that that when the building was built was to empty dirty water from all the cleaning in the basement that leads into the sewer system. It drops about 35 feet down and no longer even leads into the system anymore.

He pulls around the rear of the building with his lights and pulls in. He gets out of the vehicle, opens the overhead down and quickly jumps back into his car then drives in. Once in he closes the overhead door and goes to the back seat of his car. There he grabs a small duffle with some of his tricks of the trade. Since this was unexpected he will have to improvise. He shuts the back door and proceeds to the back of the vehicle he pops open the trunk slowly to make sure Sky High doesn't try jumping out. He is still unconscious. Lance reaches in and starts to pull out the body. He yanks hard and lets it hit the ground where he starts dragging it. The stairs, leading to the basement, are two rooms over. As he drags the body he hears the man moan and starting to come to. Lance moves quicker to get him down into the basement.

It is dark and the floor is littered with debris of all types and Lance doesn't want to make more noise he needs to. He also doesn't want to use any lights so they may not be seen from the road. He uses the light from the moon to get from room to room. He pushes the door open to the second room where he can see the door that will take him to the basement. He stops and realizes he left his straps that he would use to strangle the man in his car. He thinks about it and decides he will improvise or run back up and grab them then.

He turns the direction of the body around as he gets to the tops of the stairs here he starts pulling the body down the stairs and the man starts to awaken as his head hits every step on the way down. He nearly falls down the steps as he twists his ankle on a metal object. He recovers in time where no damage is done but the man nearly does almost come down on top of him and trip him up. He gets to the landing and from there he leaves the body which he knows the victim can't escape. He pulls out a Maglite which he turns on and sees the path to reach the room with the drain. He walks around and then starts thinking what down there can be used to kill the drug dealer. He can't find anything in the room. He enters the next room and it is filled with furniture looking like it is from the sixties and hell it probably is. He scours the ground for the drain and can't seem to find it. He sees what looks like a crack in the wooden wall, walks up to it and feels it. He thinks to himself this is the wall which hides that hidden room. He slides his fingers in the crack and runs them up and down feeling for a lever like that of a car hood after you pop it from the inside.

After trying for a few seconds he finds it and releases the latch and pushes the door inwards. He shines his light in and the smell is pungent where he decides to breathe through his mouth at first. He looks back at where he came in and listens to see if Sky High is trying to escape. Nothing. He progresses further into the room and runs the flashlight across the floor. He sees a set of steps leading down and heads to them .There it seems the room is like an old boiler room. He gets to the top of the steps and looks down. There is a couple of very old water heaters laying there destroyed. He looks and sees a couple of mice running from the rays of the light. Then he shines the light back to the left and sees a steel grate. He goes in that direction and finds the drain. He moves the grate which is very heavy .He puts his light down so he can use both hands due to the weight. After he moves it off to the left he then grabs his flashlight and shines it down the drain. He can't see the bottom and grabs a metal rod lying nearby then drops it into the drain .It takes about one to two seconds before he hears it hit water. Perfect he thinks He looks around the room and will drop the water heaters in after Sky is dropped into the drain so no one can see the body if they look down with a stronger flashlight. Lance gets back up to his feet and heads out of the room and back towards Sky.

He gets out of the room and sees Sky fidgeting around trying to get out of the restraints.

"What do you think you are doing you piece of shit?" asks Lance to Sky. Sky looks at him and tries to answer with the duct tape over his mouth.

"You stupid ass you have tape over your mouth so why are you trying to answer me? Jesus man you have all this money and no God damn brains. You are a joke." Lance leans over and grabs Sky by the back of his shirt behind his neck and drags him towards the boiler room. Sky tries squirming and kicking to the best of his ability but it gets him nowhere.

"Don't bother fighting you are just gonna get tired. You know what I was having a good night till I walk into the Giant and your big pumpkin ass has to go pushing people around because you think you are some king or something? Not in my book my man. Threatening Amy like you were. You a tough guy?" Lance stops and shines the light in his eyes and Sky tries looking away. Lance grabs his chin and forces him to look straight at the light.

"Well tough guy your time is up. All those drugs and all your little gangsta friends aren't much to you now. Maybe with you gone some of your little wanna bes will realize what they are doing and they won't end up like you on a milk carton." Lance looks into his eyes and sees the purest form of fear. Nothing better then seeing the fear come out of a person who feeds it to other people. Lance drags Sky down the steps of the boiler room and Sky is getting cut up from the trash and metal lying on the ground.

"You see Sky you try to drown people by throwing them into you pool of fear. You know the "I am going to kick your ass if you fuck with me act". Then they give in and let their neighborhood go to hell because they cower at you .You know what though. You are the coward not them you need your guns and your little buddies to incorporate this fear otherwise you have nothing. NO respect from them or for yourself. You need props to get respect and power. What's the matter no brains? Hell did you even graduate? "Sky's eyes are filled with tears that flow down his face. He starts trembling and a thumping sound can be heard from his leg shaking against one of the broken water heaters lying on the ground. Lance shines the light in that direction and back in Sky's eyes.

"You hear that? That is fear but you never heard this sound did you? It is your fear. The fear you use to have before you needed to have weapons and buddies to help you give it. Yes Sky you should be scared because I gonna kill you. You will suffer, you will pray that God has mercy and let's you pass out or die quick. I am not God I have no mercy." With that Lance smacks Sky across the face and Sky tries his damnest to scream through the tape. Lance walks away from him to about twenty feet away. Sky follows the flashlight to see what Lance is up to. He sees Lance bend over to pick up an object and sees the light coming back in his direction. Sky is shuddering in fear. Not knowing why he is there or how he will die in running through his head. He can't make out what Lance is carrying and tries his hardest to free himself but the wraps are too tight. He sees Lance stop a couple of feet away and watches Lance open up the bag. Lance unzips and looks at Sky.

"Bet you are wondering how you are going to die? Don't worry it won't be painless. I have something special for you that I thought up tonight." With that he pulls out a bottle of foam that is used to seal holes in homes from drafts or mice. He breaks off the plastic seal and inserts the straw into it. Sky can see the bottle but the light is shining in his face and he can't see what the bottle is.

"I figured I would kill you the same way you are killing people out there you sell you damn drugs to. How is that? How about since they snort shit up their nose I repay you the favor?" He looks into Sky's eyes and he sees the bloodshot eyes are overflowing with tears.

"It is too late my friend for tears. No tears now and no tears when people find out you are dead. An ingrate like you will not be missed. SO if you have a God you better pray for mercy now because in a couple of minutes you are dead." Sky tries moving as much as he can to loosen the restraints but to no avail. Lance starts to bend over and grabs Sky's head and holds it steady. Sky tries his hardest to pull away and avoid what Lance is going to do to him. Lance then positions the can towards Sky's face and shoves the straw up his nose and starts depressing the button .He can hear the foam come out and watches Sky's reaction to the foam entering his nose. He stops sending the foam in and notices Sky's is snorting it in and digesting it. He flops around on the ground struggling for air then all of a sudden his cheeks do the best impersonation of Louie Armstrong on the trumpet and he can see a yellowish liquid finding its way out between the tape and the face of Sky. It is vomit and the foam. It seems maybe not to have expanded in the nasal cavity like Lance had hoped because Sky swallowed it before it could expand and choke him. Lance throws Sky's head back towards the ground in disgust.

"You stupid bastard. You realize you are making this harder? Now you will suffer more then you had to. "With that Lance tries again sending the foam in the through the nose and he leans back. Again Sky swallows it and again vomit comes out oozing from the tape which is losing it tackiness.

"Damn it just die you piece of shit. Well guess what? You like pain then fine pain is what you are getting." Lance rips the tape off his mouth and holds his head to the ground. Sky is trying to scream but between the vomit and foam, which Lance can't tell the difference, he sounds are muffled. Sky tries biting at Lance like a dog but to no avail. Lance grabs the can and inserts the straw as far down the throat he can. He depresses the button to where Lance empties the can into his throat .The eyes are completely bloodshot if not just engorged with blood. He sees the foam expanding out of the mouth ad can see Sky trying in vain to breathe. Lance stands up and watches over the body struggle for air, for life. The body shakes and bounces around uncontrollably. Lance moves further back and shines the light down upon the mouth. He watches the foam cover half the face and realizes it looks like cauliflower growing on the face. About ten more seconds goes y and the body stops moving. He goes up to the body lying in foam, vomit, saliva, and tears. He kicks it and nothing happens. He bends over and feels for a pulse on the side of his neck and there is none. He is dead. His eyes wide open and bulging out.

Lance grabs the body and drags it towards the drain .When he gets the body there he shoves it in and the body falls. He hears the water splatter and peers down with his flashlight .He can vaguely make out the body. He wants to be safe so he grabs a two drawer filing cabinet where he throws it into the drain. He then grabs some two foot pieces of sheet metal and throws them in too. He grabs the light and looks in. He can't see anything but the garbage he just tossed in. With that he moves the drain cover back over the top and starts getting any evidence back into the bag. He takes a few minutes and grabs a rag. He then gets down and starts wiping up the footprints on the ground so they can't match them to anything. Once done he goes back over to the drain, throws the rag and the foam can down the drain. He covers it again and heads towards the stairs. His night is done. A success. An improvation. Not too bad for a spur of the moment killing he thinks to himself. He heads up the steps with the help of his flashlight. He stops abruptly halfway up the steps. He snaps his head back towards the room and hears movement.

What? He is confused he hears a loud bang. It can't be, he thinks to himself. He killed him. He turns around and heads back down the stairs at the base he stops again and hears another sound. Lance feels his heart beating through shirt. What the fuck is that sound? He starts to run towards the noises. Many thoughts go through his head. Did Sky High not die? Did he escape up the drain? How though? He runs down the last small set of stairs and shines the light in the direction of the drain. He steps closer and closer towards it and is reluctant on looking in it. He shines the light down it and can't see much. No possible way the dealer could have made this noise. He shines the light around .the room and then, again, he hears the sound but it comes from behind the drain. He elevates the beam at a steel plate against the wall. Then bang! The plate falls forwards and Lance jumps back .He catches a shadow moving from behind it. It is a rat. Lance breathes a deep sigh of relief. He shakes his head and once again heads towards the stairs.

This time he makes all the way to the garage where he opens the garage door. He gets into his car and then starts to pull out of the garage. He stops, gets out to close the door and looks around for any other headlights that may see him but the area is as dark as the darkest night. He gets back into his car and keeps the lights off. He drives through the lot's maze. He knows the area from the previous trips. He turns his lights on once he reaches the main entrance. He pulls out slowly and advances in the direction of his home. He looks at the clock. He sort of feels he has wasted his time. Yet though he would do it again. He keeps running the night through his head making sure he has not missed anything that could pin him to the murder.

From beginning to end he feels he adequately covered his tracks. Within about ten minutes he pulls into his driveway, a slight paranoia takes over him to where he looks around the street making sure he wasn't followed. Once he satisfies himself he pulls the vehicle into the garage and closes the door. He gets out and enters his house. He is tired and lets the dog out. He grabs a drink and lets the dog back. It is bed time, he had a long night. It is bad enough he has missed his woman and getting some loving he thinks to himself. He figures it is best to go right to bed.

Mason wakes up the next morning about 7am. He jumps in the shower and gets ready for work quietly. Melissa has off and he doesn't want to wake her.

He heads down the stairs and gets his lunch ready. He goes into the refrigerator and grabs the tupperware of various leftovers and preps them to take them to work. He laughs to himself remembering to bring some of the guys some leftovers.

He stands at the base of the steps heading up to the bedrooms and listens to see if Melissa is stirring. He hears nothing and just decides to head out.

He jumps into his vehicle and starts heading to work. He is happily tapping his steering wheel until he hears something on the radio. He stops tapping and listens but they change the topic. He flips to another station then another till he hears it again. He turns up the volume.

"We now have some information that the killer who has murdered five people so far. He has been labeled the Wishbone Killer due to the fact he removes two ribs from his victim and leaves them by the side of the victim. It is in a sense a calling card. Though this information is relatively new there is no hint that is has helped them get any closer to this murderer. So for now the Wishbone Killer is still evasive and the only thing they have been able to do is give him a name... I am..."

Mason slams the steering wheel with his fist. What the fuck is going on? He is pissed off at Mitchell at this moment. Did Mitchell seep the information to the press? Why would he do that? It doesn't help them out at all. No wait chill out he thinks to himself. Mitchell wouldn't do that. He decides to wait and get to the station and see how this all happened.

He approaches the station and sees the media is swarmed around the front. He proceeds to the rear. He parks his car, gets out and heads to the back door but before he can make his way in some of the media are running around the corner calling out his name. He refuses to look towards them because is he is unsure how everything came about. He yanks the door open and pulls it shut quickly as a reporter is calling his name and tugging on the door but it is locked. He looks at the mob starting to develop outside the door and hears a voice behind him.
"Whew .You made it one piece." It is agent Mitchell.

"Now before you go off on me and wonder how they received the info I will tell you. This morning we were in very early, Todd and I discussing with Ron the information you fed us last night. We discussed it and none of us knew that one of the reporters was in the room next door before he was suppose to be. Here he was let in to get a document from one of the officers and overheard us speaking about the call you made me last night. We realized it when we were watching the news fifteen minutes later and a breaking story was that. Listen we are sorry but we are pretty sure this may not damage anything we have done. Maybe it could even help us out .Maybe the publicity will make him pose for the camera and flush him out."

"Or he gets real pissed off and goes on a rampage because he does not want the pub." replies back Mason. Mitchell looks at Mason and is unsure how pissed off he is so he tries to tread lightly.

"I understand. I was pissed too but now it is too late. The only thing we can do is figure out what it is going to take to keep him from taking it to the next level every time he gets bored." They start walking together to the office discussing the situation.

"We need suspects, witnesses, anything that makes this guy think we are onto him. Right now we come up with nothing and he pokes us in the ribs, no pun intended, to annoy us." Mason says sounding a little frustrated.

"I agree. Something will happen but you need patience. Maybe we can throw a bluff out here every now and then and make him think we are making progress. It can't hurt." Mason looks at him puzzled.

"Trick him you mean?"

"Yes we have done that a couple of times and it actually had helped us once. We need to use different approaches when one does not seem to be doing us any good and Tom suggested this before this Wishbone Killer thing even surfaced today."

Mason looks at him and nods his head. "I agree let's try something who knows .What we are doing now hasn't gotten us any closer."

"Great. Now with the media we haven't decided how to address the info that was leaked. So this morning we want to see how you would think this should be handled." It is coming up on 9 o clock and they know they have about hour or two before they have a daily update with the media.

The agents and officers head into the office where they will decide what the next step will be.

"Hey Mason? Here is that notebook that still no one has claim to." Tom points out as they try to group evidence together to come up with some kind of story.

"Really? I forgot all about that notebook. It was probably the homeowners anyways."

"Actually it wasn't that was the strange part."

"How do you know that?" Mason asks Mitchell with a puzzled look on his face.

"Well because we sent it out for prints and there were none. We could find no writing in it pages were ripped out also. We did see impressions of writings on some of the blank pages like someone was writing a book."

With that Mason stops what he is doing and looks at Tom like he saw a ghost. Mason who was preoccupied with his own work asks Tom repeat what he said.

"I said it was blank but had impressions on some pages like someone was writing a book or taking notes. Why did I say something wrong?"

Mason walks towards him, takes the book and looks at it. His expression is blank almost stunned. In his head he is running a conversation he had with Marie at Burger King last week. She said" When is a book not a book?" Answer when there is no words .My god she was right but what does this mean to him?

"Hey Tom .What is today?"

"It's Thursday why?" No sooner does he answer then Mason looks at the clock it is almost lunch. He heads back to his desk and grabs his jacket.

"I gotta run. I will be back in about hour or so." Mason starts writing something down and looks at Tom. "Can you do me a favor?"

"Sure what do you need?"

"I want you to send that pad to your lab again and figure out what the words were that were written on the pages previous to that page. I have a feeling of something."

"Sure that can be done and maybe get results by the end of the day. They have double the force there to get this case done. I will call you with the info."

"You need me to come along? "Asks Mitchell worried that something is wrong.

"No I am fine I forgot I had to do something." He tries not to look desperate or excited he may have a lead but don't want to advertise it came from a soothsayer. That maybe the straw that breaks the local police department's back that their head detective gets his information for a crazy woman at Burger King on Thursdays."

"Are you sure?" Toms asks one more time.

"Yes thanks though." With that Mason rushes out the door straight to his vehicle where he speeds out of the lot like he is in a hot chase.

Mason jumps into his Durango and heads towards Burger King speeding out of the lot. A lot of information is going through his head. Now the second time she has understood something from a crime scene that she has never visited. How did this woman know this? Is this what she meant? Is this woman the killer? Maybe she knows the killer. For every angle he comes up with he comes up with another angle to that .She seems too innocent to be a person who even gets mad let alone kills. That is the reason he could not tell them where he was going or why. They would want to bring her in to say they have a lead or a suspect. Anything to calm down the public.

No deep down inside he feels maybe this woman is different. Even though he doesn't believe people who have ESP or special senses he questions this feeling now. He is about a mile away. His phone rings, it is his wife.

"Hey. Everything ok?"

"Yes why?"She responds.

"I guess just making sure .You haven't called during the day for awhile and guess I thought something was wrong."

"No I was hoping you were not busy. I just wanted to see how you were doing. Any good news today?"

He pauses but then decides to tell her what he is doing.

"Well you remember that woman who said she could see things?"

"Umm yeah?"

"Well I am going to see her. Something she said has been discovered or at least I think has been discovered at the last crime scene. This is the second time in a couple of days she has had insight on the case. "

"Do you think she is involved?" asks Melissa inquisitively.

"No but I think I should at least maybe take her a little more serious. "We have nothing, so what do I have to lose? I didn't tell the others what I was doing because it would not benefit me in anyway and they would think I am at wits end."

"Well honey it can't hurt. I don't believe in that stuff but that doesn't mean it can't happen. It could just be a coincidence or maybe she does have a gift."

"Yeah well hopefully after the way I blew her off she still talks to me."

Oh ok quick question. What makes you think she is there now?"

"She told me." Mason shoots back at first taking her tone as pessimistic. He doesn't need anyone going against him right now. He has for the first time in a long time a motivation a renewed sense for the case. He can't lose that now because of any reason.

She now can hear the anxiousness in his voice. Mason is excited, motivated and the last thing she wants to do is cast doubts on him.

"She told you?"

"I know this is crazy but she said I will be back and she is friekin right."

"Well it is lunch time maybe you will catch her."

"Honey I have a feeling I will but listen I got to go I am here now."As he pulls in he looks inside the windows hopefully catching a glimpse of her. He can't see anything so he finds the closest space and parks.

"Good luck and I love you."

"I love you too and I will call you later. Bye."

"Bye."

He shuts his cell phone and gets out of his vehicle. He heads to the front with a skip in his walk. He enters and scours the restaurant over for her. He looks at his watch and tries to recall what time he saw her last week. It is almost within an hour of the previous visit. He heads towards another part of the restaurant.

"Mr. Kade, over here" a voice calls out from the corner off to the side of the other room.

"Hi how are you? Marie right?" he starts towards her table and she gestures for him to sit.

"Yes, Good I wasn't expecting you but I am happy you are here though."

"Why is that?"

"It tells me something has come up and that I have mentioned also. Right?"

"Yes. A book, actually a notepad, was found in the latest murder. I believe the vision or whatever you called it is this. Which leads me to this. How do you know everything you know? "

"I told you I have a gift. I can see visions or moments. I can't predict the future but I can see things .Your killer's images still visits me. Sometimes he is angry with a crazed attack and another angry with a controlled anger. I can't see him only the victims or places."

"Oh and you are not just happen to be there or hear this from someone?" he then realizes how the sentence comes out and rephrases it not to offend her or make her suspicious.

"You know what I mean you don't see yourself there with him you just see through his eyes?" He feels he recovered good enough not to have offended her but it was too late.

"I am NOT your killer. You are here to interrogate me but inside you are confused. I will help you and you can decide what you want."

"You have to see this looks strange."

"I agree but time will show you."

Mason is torn between leaving and not saying anything or carrying on. He decides to ask her some questions.

"I need answers." She looks at him and can tell he has mixed feelings about this.

"What did the book look like?" she asks getting right to the point.

Mason tries to remember he has not determined if she is friend or suspect so decides to answer the questions vaguely.

"Well it was a notepad. It was empty with scribbles and words written on the page but it was impressions from a previous page. We found pages ripped out lying on the floor, crumbled up. None of the pages were the one from the previous page of the notepad. We are having trouble determining what any of this means. The writings on the ripped out pages were written by a female. Which puzzles us. We don't believe the killer is a woman but this until the prints comeback it is still open for a possibility."

He watches her body language she is stoic, just listening not showing any sides of jitters.

"It is not a female, Mr. Kade" she answers affirmatively.

"How do you know that?"

"Because you are looking for the wrong things, Mr. Kade. You will never find the paper that was on top of the one you see the impressions. There is none."

"What?!?!" Mason is puzzled and worried she is speaking like she was there and knows exactly what is going on.

"You see you are not putting the puzzle together. There are more pieces. There is a pen but it is empty, no ink. He tried to write down what he was feeling and took her pad. He found the ink was gone and could not write it down. He tried in vain to get ink out of it .he was angry, went into a rage so he threw down the pad and pen. He then continued his rage onto his victims."

Mason heads is now filled with ideas.

"Excuse me Marie I have to make a call real quick." She looks and nods. He gets up and calls Mitchell whom answers the phone.

"What's up Mason?"

"Hey Mitch did anyone bring back a pen from the crime scene with the notepad?" Mason tone is antsy and Mitch picks up on it.

"No why?"

"Do me a favor get one of my guys back there and rip the basement apart till they find a pen an EMPTY pen. Send it right in for fingerprints or DNA."

"Do you mind why I ask?"

"The killer used this notepad it was for documenting the murder. It was probably the victims. He took it because he forgot his and then used one of her pens but it was out of ink. That explains why the pages were missing and it was manhandled. As a matter of fact the pages aren't missing he had no ink so it just looks like impressions from the previous page. Which leads me to this question; did the test come back from the pad?"

"NO not yet .God knows if they even looked at it."

"I understand the fingerprints test but the dna test on the pen though." Mitchell asks trying to see where Mason s going.

"Some people when a pen runs out either roll the pen in their hands to heat up the ink in case there was an air bubble in it or others blow into the end of it trying to force the ink down the tube."

"Got it. Excellent thinking Mason but how did you come up with all this? "Mitchell asks suspiciously.

"I will explain that to you later. I am kind of pressed for time. Also if anything does show up call me and let me know." Mason tries sounding urgent to cut the conversation short to avoid answering questions.

"Will do Mason. See ya."

"See ya." With that Mason hangs up and heads back to the table where Marie is sitting.

"Sorry about that." He says trying to act naturally.

"That is ok. If I am helping you I would feel so much better and not feel like I am wasting your time by you not believing me or my information is inaccurate."

"Well time will tell." Mason says almost sounding like he trusts her in some sense. He decides to carry through asking her a few more questions.

"Has he done this with the other victims? You know recording the killings." he asks while he is taking notes.

"Yes he ..."

Mason cuts her off. "Why ??? So in other words we should go back to the other crime scenes and look for notepads or paper?!"

"NO. Listen to what I was going to say. He writes it down so maybe he can read it again when he feels a need for a fix. If he feels he needs to kill and can't at that moment he can pull it out and satisfy his desire. The notepad is his syringe and the drug are his words contained inside the book. You are wasting your time going to the other scenes. He uses a journal. He must have forgotten it and grabbed the notepad from her house. The killer brings the journal with him to the murders."

"A fix? This sounds like b.s. to me. "Mason feels angry becomes he can feel he is getting more confused then before.

"I am not a profiler .I am somewhat like a medium and see or feel things. If that assumption I had did not please you I could give you another." She stares at him with a blank stare and he looks back. He has nothing to say.

"I take it you do since you have not left here in a fit. He may like the notoriety you have given him and may be writing a book or something He may want to become even more popular a tall tale or folk lore."

"Excuse me but what the hell are you talking about? Notoriety?" he asks perturbed.

"Wishbone Killer? You have given him a name .You lead the news every night with *The Wishbone Killer this or The Wishbone Killer that"* I can feel a satisfaction or joy he gets. Yet at the same time I get an anger coming from him. Again like I said before he is perplexing sometimes I feel he does not know himself or who he is. Remember you and the media gave him that distinction. He may do the unthinkable and cash in on something like this and even insult the intelligence of man even more."

Mason digests everything she says and realizes that some of this makes sense to him. He wants to stop and try to get back to the matter at hand.

"Why did you not tell me this before? I mean the notepad. If you knew about the notepad and journal why wait?"
"Because if my images are wrong and mislead you then that time could have been used for real clues. "

"Are there any more images? You know." Mason stops and can't believe he asked that but he does not completely believe her yet. Maybe he should take her down to the station.
"I haven't seen anything that can help but there is more. He is not done. His appetite is increasing. More pain will come but I am scared to say I don't feel any relief coming Mr. Kade, this WILL last for some time. You need to be open minded." She reaches for her drink then sets it down and reestablishes her stare." I said last time you will be tested in all ways and you are being tested right now. He is leaving you a message. A game maybe, I am not quite sure. My visions maybe advantageous to you .This could give you a leg up if it is possible. "
"A game? With me?"
"Maybe .Maybe he is bored and needs to challenge your or the authorities into catching him. I do know this he is extremely intelligent. He can almost

split his thoughts; the killer is at smart as two men. Complex I feel. Every time I have an image or thought then the next one convolutes the previous one."

Mason looks at his watch. He is anxious to go back to the last scene, look for the pen and maybe print it. Part of him still thinks he is wasting time with her. Questions still arise about her knowledge.

"I have to get going, Marie. I have a lot to do." He stands up and looks at her.

"It is C-a-n-t-o-u-r Mr. Kade."

He looks at her with a perplexing look.

"I know you will look me up and make sure you eliminate me as a suspect. So I am making sure you spell it right."

"Uh thanks. "He replies awkwardly. He looks at her embarrassed like she can read his mind. "Take care." He walks away and reaches for his keys in his pocket.

"See you soon Mr. Kade."

With that he walks out the door. He pauses and turns around and looks back at her. He can't believe he is about to do what happens next. He walks back in and approaches her again and reaches in his pocket.

"Did you forget something or are you coming back to arrest me?" she asks with a light hearted chuckle.

"Actually I want to give you my business card so if you have anymore dreams or visions you can call me at anytime. I don't care how minute it maybe but I do appreciate it." He can't believe this but he has a feeling she has a little more to her then what he originally thought. She takes the card from him and puts it into her purse.

"I don't have these every night I go to sleep so don't expect a call tomorrow. They happen when they happen."

"I understand. Again have a good day and thanks for you time."

"Likewise I will take advantage of your offer Mr. Kade."

Mason nods, smiles and again heads out of the restaurant. He notices he actually trusts her to a degree.

Heading to his car he feels like maybe she is onto something regardless if it is a gift or maybe even a guess but she somewhere is making some of this make sense.

Yet how does he bring any of this up at the station? The feds will look at him like he is the crazy one. He feels he has earned some creditability from Mitchell and Tom. They don't seem to leave him in the cold nor do they act like his input on the case is irrelevant. He now has to decide what to tell them, he or actually Marie is saying. Maybe he can just say it is him but then at some point it will probably blow up in his face.

He looks at his watch and realizes it has been over an hour and nothing about a pen has popped up. He gets in his car and takes off. He decides to head to the crime scene and look for the pen himself or at least assist. He is at least optimistic which is the best feeling he has had for awhile in this case.

He arrives at the scene in ten minutes and is greeted by some of the team. No one has found the pen he is looking for. He turns over everything all over the house looking through drawers, under beds anywhere he can think a pen maybe. While he was on the second floor he hears footsteps behind him and turns around. It is Mitchell.

"Hey what's up?" asks Mitchell as he enters the room holding a folder.

"Nothing just figure I would swing by and show you the file. The results came back and there is not a whole to build off of." With that Mason gets up and takes the file from Mitchell and opens it anxiously. Part of him hoping to find a clue for the case another part of him hoping to set his mind at ease with Marie, give her some credibility. He glances over the folder and the papers inside. The results show the words that are legible sad,

> " Watching the two squirm in the web I have spun and has my head feel a high that makes me feel like I will pass out. I will drain their evil from them to where it flows on the floor till no evil exists in their bodies. Then people will realize how serious I am. I will puncture their bodies with holes to let the evil flow as fast as it can out of them. I will watch the pain till they are lifeless or I pass out from the euphoria. The bitch is pissing herse"

That is all it says .There are notes made that state there are scribbles near the bottom of the page. As Mason reads on Mitchell sifts through some paperwork on the desk in the room glancing over to Mason waiting for him to finish reading the report.

Mason doesn't see much to build off of but does now know that somehow Marie is a person whom can help.

Mason also notices a paragraph stating that the pen used did have ink and the impressions are from a previous page on top of the current. Which means the page on top is missing .Then there is a chance that page maybe in the house.

He looks up at Mitchell. "Did you see this? There could be a page lying around that was the previous page to this."

"Yes I saw that. I told the team up my way up here to look for that page."

"Great thanks. Here there is not that can do for me anymore." Mitchell grabs it from Mason. He looks at him and you can tell something is bugging him.

"Mace can we go outside and talk? Alone?"

"Yeah sure what is up?" Mason follows Mitchell downstairs to out front where no one is. He can tell something is wrong but he can't put his finger on it. They get outside and approach the front of Mitchell's vehicle where he turns around and faces Mason.

"Listen is there something you want to tell me?" he asks Mason almost gently not to offend him. Mason now knows what is going on.

"Oh this is about how I have received some of my info isn't it?"

"Yes. I am not upset but this person maybe crucial to the investigation and there maybe stuff you don't know about him that we may."

Mason can now see instantly what agent Mitchell is going to say without going any further.

"Well I was going to tell you but you need to understand why I needed to keep this quiet. First her name is Marie Cantor and."

"Her?"

"Yes. She says she is a medium like a person who can see things. I know this is going to sound crazy but I met like a couple weeks ago and she approached with what I thought was bullshit. For a week I gave her thoughts no credibility till the bones incident. After that she then mentioned the notepad."

"Ok so this woman approaches you tells you things about the crime scenes, they pan out and you didn't feel it was important to fill us in?" Mitchell asks trying not to sound confrontational.

"I did look into her background and she came up clean. At worst I thought she was crazy but I am not sure about that anymore. I didn't know how the team would take their info coming from a whacko. Or if they would feel offended someone not part of the case is giving them more leads then people inside. I hope you understand." Mason is worried and not sure what is next to come out of agent Mitchell's mouth.

"Well if you have the info about this woman we will do a background and eliminate her from the list. Maybe she can help us since it seems she has helped twice already."

"That is fine. I have the info in my truck and I will give it to you before I go. Are we fine?" He hopes Mitchell has understood exactly what and why he has done what he done.

"Of course. I understand. I would have felt the same way but you should not have sat on it as long as you had because it could have jeopardized or slowed down our progress. I am going to head off though. There are a couple of stops I need to make. I guess see you at the office in a couple of hours?"

"That sounds good. I am going to head back in and see if I can help them out."

With that they part ways both in the back of their head hoping Marie is the wild card they need.

It is Tuesday of the following week and Lance is coming home from work. There is a report of a missing woman from the area and he is suspicious why there is no much false information being passed around. He doesn't know to whether to believe this report of a missing woman. He is also disgusted from the report about the Wishbone Killer. He dwells on why a nickname has been given and suspects them to try to draw him out .He heard about all day since his office is close to the lunchroom where the television was in MSNBC and there seemed to be no stop of the coverage. He was more then excited to get outside. He gets in his car and listens to the radio. He finds a station that is playing a song he likes and he doesn't let what he believes is mind games the feds are playing, into his head. He lets his mind drift he has about 10 minutes to be home. He debates if he wants to buy dinner or just make something at home. After thinking about it he decides to save some money and just go home. Hell he can prepare something maybe he'll make some chicken parm. After dinner he thinks he may run out and rent a movie. No television tonight he has had enough from earlier.

Lance arrives home from working out and walks in the house. He smells some food and is curious where it is coming from since she is not to be home for at least another hour. He walk around the corner into the dining room and sees the table is set.

"What?" he says and at that moment the kitchen door swings open and she is standing there with a plate in her hands.

"Hi honey, I wanted to surprise you and make you a nice dinner. Surprised?"

"Um yes but I thought you had to work late till 7?"

"I left early the shift had enough people to cover so I thought I would do something nice for you. I made your favorite to, chicken parm." She set his spot and has a big smile on her face. This is what he always wanted, a woman who wanted to do something for him for no reason like he does for others.

"Wow! Boy am I special or what?" He walks towards her and embraces her. He gives her a kiss on her lips and looks into her eyes.

"I have to be the luckiest guy in the world."

"Maybe you are" she says with a smile."Also I have dessert for you too."

"Really what did you buy?"

"Honey I don't have to buy this dessert but it is your favorite." She smiles devilishly. Oh boy he knows it is going to be a good night.

"Well can I help you finish?"

"Sure if you want babe. Grab the drinks?"

He heads towards the kitchen and stops by the television for a breaking story. A reporter is in town and reporting a missing girl has been found. Just then she walks in the room.

"Did you hear about that? That little girl was missing for two hours and that crazy bum at the Wal-mart had her."

"WHAT?" Lance replies angrily.

"Yeah a ten year old girl was missing around the shopping center near Wal-mart and they had search crews out and then she was found nearby in an abandoned house but while police were there the bum never came back and they couldn't arrest him. She was harmed but they are not saying how nor are they saying if the guy did it because she is too scared to answer."

Lance is pissed one thing that eats at him is child abductors, sex predators or child killers.

"Did they know where he is at?"

"Not that I am aware but someone was saying there is not enough evidence without her pointing him out to convict him. Originally the thought it might have been the Wishbone Killer but no one thought he was a child killer."

With that it hits Lance. First now his girlfriend is using the Wishbone Killer title and now he was associated with a child killer. His mood shifts but knows he must hide it till a later time. He heads towards the television and turns it off.

"Let's have a nice dinner he says to her."

"And a great dessert "she says smiling back.

He is bothered by what he has seen and what may be assumed but for now he must put that on the back burner. He looks up at her and feels a decision must be made about his life and this incident was the event to catapult him into his life altering change. He grabs a drink out of the fridge and kisses her as he walks by to his seat.

"You are special" he says.

"Thank you." She rubs his back as he walks by.

They sit down and start to eat.

It is 1115 and Lance lays next to her naked .The dinner was great and they went for a walk after dinner. They just finished having sex and good sex at that .She is breathing heavy next to him and pulls him in tight to her body.

"I love you babe" she says quietly into his ear as she kisses his neck. "You make me feel so special .I enjoy the idea of getting old with you. That is the thought I enjoy waking up to."

With that comment a punch to his sternum is delivered. At that moment Lance realizes he wants the same thing he reflects on all the times and experiences they shared and there is nothing he would change.

"I am so happy you feel that way too honey. I love you and can't wait till the time when I am going to the store to get your Depends.' She pinches his skin and they laugh.

"There is nothing more I could want from someone that you don't have."They kiss passionately for a second and she falls back into his arm.

Lance lays there and comes to the conclusion his killing is done. He can't keep this up and tie down with her. This is it no more. With the thought earlier that he was associated as a child killer then her comments and his feelings is apparent the time has come. With the thought that his future children or any child would be in fear because of his killings is not what he wants. The police do not know his motive and as far as he is concerned they may think he is sick enough to kill or abduct a child and that is where the line is drawn. It hit him hard when she said earlier that they thought he was a suspect .Never did he ever want to give that perception. It is over.

So now does he just stop killing out of the blue? Yes he could do that, he thinks, but then it always leaves open the possibility of the cops finding out down the road somehow .Either by persistent investigation or just the sake of the case of having no closure.

So how does he end it and all the investigation and start his life over with the woman of his dreams?

He lays there and runs through scenarios and then comes up with one.

He will frame someone who deserves it. It will take work but Lance can feel excited that he has come up with a solution to resolve it deserves it more then John Smythe, the bum. That is who he will frame. Anyone who goes after a child doesn't deserve to live. Chances are he will strike again so Lance will put an end to his killing and get the child pervert off the street.

He looks over at her and gives her a kiss on her forehead and pulls her close. He knows his effort for the next few days will be his escape from what some may call a monster inside. Time will be an issue so he will have to come up with a plan and make sure it is air tight like his murders if this is to work. This won't be simple. Hell I am going to start right now he thinks to himself .He is tired. He needs all his energy to come up with a plan tomorrow so he closes his eyes and slowly drifts off to sleep

.

Mason and Mitchell drive through town and it is about 530 pm. The streets are bare. The town, the area is living in fear. Only people out are those going to their car or those getting paid to be out. What has happened? He looks over at Mitchell and notices the same sympathetic glare out of his eyes also.

"Scary isn't it?" says Mitchell.

"What's that?"

"Death is like a virus it eats the community from the inside out. When I first came here people were out shopping and living yet they may have been scared but over the course of a few weeks everything has changed. The virus was alive just not visible and now it has showed its ugly head." A serious tone has overtaken his demeanor. Mason looks at him and sees a concern. "Look no one is out and those who are are speed walking to their cars just to avoid being snatched. This is what the whole area and neighborhoods look like ghost towns. Reminds me of the DC sniper when people would get gas and duck while they were getting it.'

"Yeah I remember that. That was messed up. "Mason pauses for a second as he turns to head to the northern part of town.

"Can I ask you a question and get a honest answer?" Mason asks almost reluctantly.

"Sure have I lied before?"

"No I just know the nature of this question may provoke an indirect answer or possibly a lie."

"No problem, shoot."

"Why do you seem worried or am I misreading you?"

"It is god damn day light out and people are scared. That my friend is what concerns me."

"I know why but why to the severity you show it. People move out concern you?"

"Not people, him. What if his job was to scare society to the point they never come out? Maybe that is his goal then carries on somewhere else. Then all this work is wasted and society could never rest till they know he is captured. Then a new neighborhood, a town, a society goes through what these people have. A big circle."

"You're scaring me Mitch; almost sounds like you don't think we will catch him." Mason starts to get a sick feeling. All he has worked on, the feelings and confidence that was starting to grow like they were getting somewhere is now sinking and sinking fast.

"This guy is good. We are having trouble with developing a profile. When that happens it is hard to narrow the field down. He is killing at a rapid pace. Not like some serial murderers it is once a month or longer, this guy is trying to get to a pace or every few days forget the weekly or monthly shit. We may have a bored serial murderer and that scares me quite a lot."

"Hey we are further then we were before you guys arrived. We now know why he does the broken ribs and the notebook. Now we can focus on possible victims." It now seems like Mason is the strong confident one at this point looking over at Mitchell trying to make eye contact and support.

"Right –the whole town. Remember we can't figure the similarities? Also our best witness is a fuckin soothsayer. Step back and look this. We are not in good shape at this point. There is a woman missing, dead people, a little girl sexually abused and we have god damn nothing!! " he says angrily as his eyes scour the streets for anything.

Mason feels awkward. His friend Marie is now told by the feds she is not worth the stories she tells. He feels obligated to dig Mitch out of the quagmire of negativity.

"We still have the bum. He did the girl and the woman goes missing a day and a half later. He has a good of suspect as any."

"Mace our bum is our only suspect. Honestly do you think he is capable of these other killings? The guy has no car so how does he get around? How is not seen? He has done one crime but I can't accept he is the killer. Our guy is smart very smart. He is always checking himself for errors. He is methodical. He doesn't give us much to work with. He now gives us clues because he is getting uninterested. Who knows maybe another reason he goes elsewhere is to find new people to play his game and give him a challenge. He maybe so smart he has made errors and we still can't catch them."

"I know but he is all we have so let's pray he is it and we find him. " Mason pauses and makes sure he words his following statements without sounding like an ass.

"Also Marie, the woman has deciphered a few things ,she has helped so regardless of what we believe of her she makes sense a little .I have no clue how but she is clean so maybe is she doesn't have a sense then she is a good guesser."

Mitchell realizes his tantrum has gotten to Mason's confidence. "Hey man I didn't mean to insult you or rip down your efforts of you and your men. Hell my men haven't done much either and we are suppose to be the pros that's why we were called in. In reality I was embarrassed to say what we know is from your friend and not from our own research."

"No need to apologize. We are all stressed out. We will get him. It is just a matter of time". Time is of the essence. The longer this goes the longer society will suffer. Society may never be the same again even after they catch him. Any murder after this will destroy any repairing that time has healed. Surely every murder after this will have some portion of society thinking "Oh God another serial murder?" Mason can see the cycle happening causing pain again and again. This is going to be a long healing process he can feel.

"You bet we will". Mitch says with a tone of optimism as he slams his fist into his hand. With that they look at each and simultaneously hit their fists together as a sign of agreement and partnership.

Lance wakes up the following morning and heads to kitchen to make breakfast. He grabs a bowl of cereal, heads into his office and starts outlining a plan for his exit. Last night while he was sleeping he came up with a few rough drafts but then he forgot them. He knows he has to move quickly but yet be thorough so he doesn't get caught. He thinks to himself how bad would that be he gets caught get out of killing but never while he was doing it. He starts writing on a pad and paper. He stops, gets up and turns the television on. He heads towards the remote and brings it back to his desk. The local news is on and what a surprise the focus is on the serial killer. He has had enough and changes the station .He stops at a national all news station with a reporter trying in vain to make a link to the bum and the Wishbone Killer.

"There are leads linking the homeless man to being Wishbone Killer an inside source states." The volume goes down and the station changes. Lance thinks what a crock .Links. No god damn links when the bum is not the killer. Wishbone Killer. All this bullshit .All they are trying to do is draw me out with inaccurate information. Screw them I am done. They want this homeless man the Wishbone Killer then that is what they will get. Hell he probably has taken this other woman so the set up shouldn't be too hard to believe. He stops writing on his pad and tears up the paper he started writing on. Maybe I should do this on my computer. He thinks how he can hide the file so not even the police or his fiancé will find it if anything ever went wrong. He also has software that is hacker's grade that will encrypt it.

He sits back and starts thinking. He wants to link the plan to at least one past murder but how. He doesn't want to visit any of the victim's sites. Too risky. He taps his head with his fingers almost hoping to wake up some ideas for himself.

He grunts to himself this could take awhile. He looks at the clock and it is almost 9am. He turns on Sportscenter.

Jill went out for breakfast with a couple of her fellow workers so she won't be there for another hour or so. While he watches TV he realizes he needs to go to the store for some stuff for the house. He gets up grabs his keys, wallet and heads out.

He thinks, as he is driving, that he is going to need a couple of things to carry out his plan which is in the rough draft stages but the material is pretty much the constant.

He arrives at Wal-mart in about ten minutes or so and heads into the store. He grabs a cart and does his weekly shopping

Water, dog food, house cleaners and some snacks. He heads to the hardware aisle and grabs a bag of the big tie wraps and a roll of duct tape. There he thinks to himself I have everything I need and looks at his watch. It is almost 10 and Jill should be home soon. He goes to the check out and the self serve ones are not in service so he looks for the shortest line and gets in it.

He is next person up and puts his items on the conveyor. He looks at the magazines at the register while waiting his turn. He is up. He puts the magazine away and is greeted by the young cashier.

"How are you today?"

Lance looks up and realizes it is the young man who was scolded by Lance's scapegoat, Charles Cleters.

"Oh hey. I am good you?"

"I am fine. A little busy since the self serve is down." Lance likes the guy. He seems a little quirky but hell isn't everyone at that age.

"Weekly shopping?"

"Yes I have time so I decided to get it done now."

"Yeah, I see people weekly and pretty much know this list by a few trips. "

"Oh really. "

"Yes I know you because you are the only person who buys the big bag of ties and duct tape. What are you doing with that? "At that moment Lance is thrown off at what to say. The look on the cashier's face is inquisitive. Not sure if he is being interrogated or just a blank statement. "Tying the kids down?" With that he laughs. Lance feels a relief come upon him. For a second he was unsure where it was going.

"Well you know when they get out of hand it is the only way."

"Little rug rats gotta love them though." Lance feels better and jokes around with the guy.

"No kids here not yet. I just am doing duct work in my house and need this stuff."

"Sure that is what they all say. Well your bill is $21.88. Credit or debit." The clerk laughs heartily at his own joke.

"Credit is fine." Lance swipes his card and then heads out. Whew that was weird. He heads out and looks for Smythe but does not see him. Hopefully when he does need to find him he is there. Once again if Smythe does something stupid and gets caught then there goes the escape route.

Before he gets into his car he takes one more look around the lot for Smyhte and does not see him. He reassures himself nothing is wrong and the bum is probably picking out the trash out back. He wasn't arrested because they did not have enough on him since the girl would not speak.

He ponders what if he does get arrested then what? How bad will that be? He stops instantly thinking that. He needs to use his energy for positive thoughts not for some garbage.

He heads back to the house and thinks about picking up some roses for his girlfriend to lay them on the bed next to her so when she awakens she will see them. He takes the long way home so he can think and maybe driving around will give him ideas of places he may need to access or use to finish this deed.

Mason is sitting at home with the agents and his wife discussing the case. He looks at the clock and it is about 630 and he is quite hungry.

"Hey Mitch are you guys hungry?"

"Actually I am good how about you Todd?"

"I guess I could eat something." He replies.

"Hey hun what are you hungry for?" Mason asks her.

"Don't care .Why don't you guys decide what you want and then I will pick from there."

Mason looks over at Mitch and they nod in agreement.

"Hell I guess I can get something. Do some hoagies?" states Mitchell.

"Ok let me get the menu." Mason heads out of the room then comes back in and hands the menu to the agents who decide what they want along with Melissa.

"Hey Mason you order and we will go to pick it up. There are some files I want to bring back and we can review." Mitchell then reaches for his jacket and Tom gets up too. They head towards the door.

"Ok sounds good. I will tell them you will be there in about 20 minutes then?" Mason asks as he goes towards the phone.

The agents look at each other and agree. They head out the door and Mason makes the call and places the order. He walks back in the direction of the cradle for the phone and as he sets it in its place the phone rings. He looks at the Caller ID but does not recognize the name or the number. He answers it.

"Hello?"

"Mr. Kade?" asks the voice which he recognizes instantly it is Marie. His heart races. He knows she would only call if something came to her which of course makes him anxious.

"Marie, how are you? "

"I am fine. Am I interrupting your dinner?"

"No we are eating in a little bit. Is something wrong?" He tries not to sound over anxious.

"Actually this maybe nothing but I have been getting visions but they are inconsistent but they are happening at a more frequent pace." She says it in a tone that makes Mason excited.

"What is it?" he asks anxiously.

"Last night, which was my latest vision, keeps having objects but they are all over the place. I can't piece them together and I hope somehow they help you. Just like the other visions I would hope this can help."

"That is fine let's try and see if any of it can make sense." Mason tries assuring her and heads out of the dining to his office. He shuts the door then sits down, grabs a pen and paper.

"Ok these have happened more then once but they do not occur in any special order. I see a hutch like in a dining room. The room seems small and messy."

"Is it in a house? Anything that can tell us something more?" Mason asks.

"No I can't tell anything more for you but there is something blue or green that comes up like a curtain I think. I also feel a discomfort when I have this vision. An uneasiness. I feel pain, Mr.Kade. I can't wait till the vision passes. It is the first time I have felt this since these visions have occurred." Her voice is shaky; Mason can tell she is frightened.

"Ok Marie. Take your time. Take a deep breath. When you are ready, continue or if you want finish the thoughts." Mason sounds like Dr. Phil but he doesn't want her to stop. Even though everything she has said has meant nothing but if the past has proven anything the future will reveal the answers.

"I think this room is where he tortures his victims. I can't explain but that is the only thing I come up with. I don't see any people in this vision. I do se chains though but I am not sure what they are used for. Then there are numbers they are seven, three, three .When these numbers appear then I feel a calm come about me."

"Maybe this is an address. Maybe all this is where he lives. Seven thirty three. I think..." Mason is interrupted by her.

"No they don't always appear like that actually the most common sequence is three, three, and seven. "

"Oh, ok." Mason says with somewhat of a letdown in his voice.

"I know what I am telling is not the best info but it has to mean something somehow." Marie sounds disappointed also.

"I am sure it does we just need to wait to figure it out." Mason doodles the numbers trying to think somehow what these numbers mean. He decides to change the topic for a little maybe helping jog one of their memories.

"So Marie when did you realize you have this special gift?" Figuring it was a good personal question maybe it would give her a reassuring feeling about herself.

"Well it was when I was thirteen and I was at my job at the pharmacy. It was 603 when I looked at the clock on the microwave. I remember this vividly because I was talking to my friend Jennifer and we were laughing when all of a sudden a feeling struck me of sadness. I was gasping just to speak when then I looked at the clock. I immediately stopped talking and knew I had to get home. I ran home and was greeted at the door by my father. He said he was looking for me and I asked why. He told me my mother was in an accident and we needed to get to the hospital. I asked him what time did this occur and he told me around 6 o'clock. I then realized that feeling I felt was my mom in pain from the accident. After that I paid attention to everything from being able to predict when someone was about to come over to when something was going to happen in the news in the area."

"Wow were you scared?"

Mason looks out his window and sees the agents are back. He realizes he may have to rush this otherwise he has to explain everything. He wants to keep this quiet till he can sort any of it out like before.

"Well listen Marie if anything else pops up call me. I will see if I can put any of this together. "

"No problem Mr. Kade but one last thing."

"What is that?" He asks as he puts the pad and pen away in the drawer. He can hear the car doors shut outside.

"When I have the visions of the numbers I see it differently."

"How is that?"

"Well this is strange but everything is like red. Like I am looking through sunglasses. When this happens I feel peace. I feel tranquil."

"Hmmn. That is strange but if it is like your other thoughts hopefully it will take us somewhere." Mason hears voices out in the foyer and decides to cut the conversation short so the agents don't get suspicious.

"Well Marie I will look into this and I appreciate your effort. I do have to go though, not trying to be rude." He tries rushing the conversation to avoid dealing with questions from the agents.

"I understand Mr.Kade. I called because these are different and hope they can help."

"Me too. Good night Marie and thanks again."

"Your welcome and good night." With that they hang up . Mason pauses for a second and thinks over what she said but he can't for more then a second because the agents are calling for him to come and eat. He turns off the light in the office and has all night to digest what he had just heard.

It is 830pm and Jill is getting ready to leave for work early. Someone has called in sick and she volunteered to cover some of the hours till her shift is due. Lance walks towards her with a bag in his hand.

"What is this?" she asks.

"Your lunch babe. I figured I had a little time to kill and since you were leaving early for work I would help you out."

"Awwww. I knew there was a reason I love you. Granted sometimes you act a little quirky and act like a contrarian."

"I do it because it makes you smile."

"No you do it to torture me .Well whatever the reason thank you .I got to run I want to get a drink on the way in." She leans towards him and gives him a kiss. "I can't wait till you are all mine." She whispers in his ear. "I am, babe."

She looks at her hand and laughs. "Not according to my hand I am."

"You are so funny babe. Hurry hustle." She grabs her phone and pats Traegen on his head on the way out her door.

Lance stands at door and watches her pull away. He thinks how long is night ahead is. He closes the door and the dog follows him inside. He heads to the basement to get his bag of tools for his final job. He heads towards his office, sits at his desk and looks over his notes. He runs it through his head. It seems like it is foolproof but not knowing what different factors he may run into he is aware he may have to improvise at any given moment. His bag is packed and it is just a matter of everything being where it should be. He looks at the clock it is 845 and figures he has all night.

He then erases the file and shuts down the computer he knows what needs to be done. The blueprint to start the rest of his life is embedded in his mind. He heads upstairs and reaches into the rear of the closet for a bag. Inside the bag are clothes he bought just for this night. At the end of the night he plans on throwing away all the clothes that he will wear this night, gloves too. This is the last night he will kill and wants nothing to remind of his past let alone help get him caught. He changes into a black sweatshirt; his black sweat pants and sneakers with his normal leather gloves. He goes downstairs and puts his bag next to the garage. He walks into the kitchen, reaches for the dog food and feeds Traegen. He goes into the refrigerator and has some left over pasta. Maybe it is his nerves or the excitement from knowing what he finally wants and being so close to starting that life with his girlfriend Jill. He is never nervous when it comes to killing .Tonight though either it is nerves or the anticipation of ending it all. Usually he is impervious to that feeling for he is so passionate about what he does he has no doubts or regrets.

He grabs the meal out of the microwave, sits down and starts to eat. He runs through the plan through his head one final time before he heads out. He has only one decision that he has yet to make and that is to either plant evidence to lead the authorities to him or make an anonymous call on the day he finalizes his plan. He has figured he will probably do both.

He gets back up and grabs a drink then sits down. He checks outside because he hears a noise and maybe he is a little paranoid since the dog isn't even barking.

First, he heads to Charles Cleters house and parks at the mall lot which is about half a mile away. He will then walk to Cleters house. There he will scope out the house before entering it and kidnapping Cleters. He will in the process leave some planted evidence to lead the police and feds to where Cleters will be. He can't make it look too evident though but one piece will be who did it and the other piece will be where Cleters could possibly be found. Granted one piece will only be significant to an agent who is alert or maybe an officer familiar with the area. Lance has done his homework and paid attention to how scrupulous these guys are. He feels they will catch the clues otherwise his anonymous phone will absolutely have to be made.

He will lead Cleters to Cleter's car and take the car to the warehouse where he can park it in a garage that has an entrance in the rear of the building that not many people are familiar with. Then he ties him up and contains him till he gets John Smythe to the warehouse where he will kill Cleters first then have the cops come out where John Smythe will be there in a rage where, if it goes right he will be killed before any information is dispersed from him. So much depends on timing. So many questions he has gone through to make sure he has covered all angles.

What if Cleters is not there? He will wait and if it doesn't happen tonight then he will go to his back up plan. No Mr. Cleters will not get away with some type of disturbance from Lance. He figures he will steal his car and use that as part of the setup. At least that way he can draw his name into the whole serial murder investigation and cause him some grief since he can't kill him at that time. He just has to walk back to the mall, get his vehicle and call it a night. Tonight one of the two plans MUST happen. One for Lance's sake and because time is important in this situation John Smythe can not do something else stupid. He can't get arrested where he can't set him up. Then it is back to square one. At that point unless he can come up with someone else that is believable then so be it otherwise maybe he stops cold but the authorities will never stop hunting him down. He will always be looking over his shoulder because there will be no finality to the case for the victims or the authorities. How bad would it be if he has children then one day their daddy gets arrested for being a murderer and at that time he will be weaved as a Friday the thirteenth character and not ,as what he sees himself as ,an advocate for the small helpless people.

He is halfway done his meal and thinks of an area in the warehouse where Cleters will be held. He has all the material to contain him for a few days but he plans on keeping him there for a couple of days then gets Smythe to the warehouse. He hopes from when Smythe gets there till when the authorities show up he hopes is 15 minutes window. The most critical part is to get Smythe to run at the authorities like a nut and get himself killed. At that moment he must be out of the warehouse when they swarm it. He plans on doing this by running through an underground tunnel that was made during 1776 it runs about 1500 yards out by the river where the door is covered over the last forty years when the owners at that time decided to shut the tunnel down for safety of the children in the area. He has gone to the site and made sure the door is accessible and can be opened .He kept the brush over it to keep it camouflaged. Then he will head towards a park where his car will be parked and leave from there. He will head straight home and be able to catch it all on the news.

He has money set to the side to give to Smythe which is how he will lure him to the warehouse. He will convince Smythe he owns the warehouse then get him to come and work on cleaning it up. The reason he will tell him, he is hiring Smythe is because he is giving him less money then other people and he wants to save money. He knows where Smythe sleeps which is in a secluded area where no one will see the meeting happen and can't pin Lance to Smythe in anyway. There the time will be setup close to that meeting ,the next day actually, so Smythe does not have time to interact with anyone and tell them where he is going or what is doing so it has to happen late at night and have Smythe meet in the early am.

Funny he thinks to himself he prides himself on being methodical and error free but now he must incorporate a plan where he shows he makes a mistake to him it is harder to come up with a plan with mistakes then it was with one that didn't have any. Somehow he has to make it look like the killer is getting sloppy or maybe just had some oversights. .Hymm, that's doable he concludes.

He finishes his meal and washes the dishes. He lets Traegen out and goes over the equipment in his bag that he will need that night. Time is near. He lets the dog in and starts taking the bag to the car. He gets to the garage door and looks bag at Traegen who is looking at him from the kitchen.

"Well boy this is it. Be good. Wish me luck." With that he heads out the door. He gets in his vehicle and starts it .He grabs the gear shift then hesitates. His feelings are not that of typical murders. It is different he realizes. He is focused.

He is happy, tonight is the night he puts an end to the so called "Wishbone Killer". With that he shifts into reverse and heads out. He has a warm feeling and he will make some people happy in return. Just as long as he does not get caught.

About fifteen minutes later Lance pulls up into the mall lot and parks his car towards the rear of the lot but still blending in with other cars. He makes sure no one is coming to their cars or pulling in around him so he can get out of his vehicle unnoticed .The mall is behind on their security and there are no cameras so he is safe and can't get tracked there. He reaches around and grabs his bag of supplies, gets out of car and heads toward the rear where the woods are that will take him to Cleter's house.

He makes his way and within fifteen minutes or so he will be there. Even though he is a barren area he still maintain as much silence so not that he can be heard but so he can hear anyone in the area. Never know when some couple wants to come out for an inconspicuous rendezvous and there he is dragging a body through their makeshift bedroom.

"Uh excuse me", he pictures himself saying to the couple as they look at the body he is carrying. "Mine wasn't as agreeable to come as yours." He laughs to himself as he plays the scenario in his head.

So quiet. Kind of eerie thinking how if this was a movie the background and setting would be perfect. As he walks he tries to take notice if the path he is taking will be easily recognizable for clues if he should leave any such as footprints. He made sure his pockets were empty so no incriminating evidence would be left behind.

Lance is about ten minutes away. He can't see any house's lights in the near distance but he can hear some dogs barking. Maybe it at the full moon. He is using the light being supplied by the full moon that is poking in and out of the trees.

He starts to think back when he was a boy and he would walk the woods from his friend's house and see if he could see some wild animal. He remembers one night hearing some crying and movement through the brush where he was walking and went to check it out. He came across an injured animal. From a distance it looked like a cat of some type from the mountains, in his mind at least, but it was a young fox. He remembers approaching not knowing who was scared more. He pulled out his superhero flash light to get a better look and saw it's foot was caught in a trap. He knows that some hunters would lay small traps to stop or slow down a deer so they could kill it. They always picked up the traps so no people would get caught or hurt but in this case they must have forgotten.

He slowly put out his hand to show friend to the fox and the fox seemed to understand. At that point Lance knew he was to help the fox and felt they were supposed to meet. After comforting it for a few minutes he opened the trap being careful not to get hurt himself. Once he did he took the fox home and stayed up till 3 that night caring for the fox. Using two paint stirrers for sides of a splint he wrapped it bandage adhesive and let it sleep in his garage where he made it a bed by laying the recycling bin on it's side , putting a couple of towels and pillow in it.

He remembers arguing with his dad about keeping it because it was friendly but his dad insisted that it was taken out of its natural environment. It wasn't happy, he said, but funny Lance thought because after that point the fox seemed to never leave his side. Of course when he was hungry he would let Lance know by scratching the side of Lance's leg. He would in return get dog food, which he devoured. The fox actually behaved like a dog. It would get a stick that was thrown and bring it back. Never barked though reminsces Lance as he chuckles. The fox played with Lance and followed him around wherever he went. Hell he remembers leaving the garage door open one day and the fox wouldn't leave. It just stayed around waiting for Lance to come out. Finally though Lance finally took the fox out to the woods far from his house after a year of having him when his dad explained to him that maybe the fox wanted to be a daddy and couldn't be because Lance was preventing him from doing so. That is when the birds and bee speech came out. An appropriate time when it was thought about. His dad said that maybe it was time for Buddy to have his own family and unlike a dog they couldn't just go out and mate him with another dog. The argument lasted five minutes when Lance's best answer was go catch another fox and bring it back to the house.

A couple of problems though. One can't just catch a fox unless they trap it and Lance refused to think of doing a trap like the one that caught Buddy. Couldn't go to the store and just buy one so the only option left was to let it free. Lance thought about that long and hard for a night to finally conclude his dad was right.

He decided the next day he would part ways. It was a tough decision but him and his dad took the fox to the woods where Lance said his final goodbyes. He realized that day for something good to happen that sometimes something bad had to precede it He drove him with his dad and it was a quiet ride. At ten years old he for the last year learned a lot. Responsibility comes in different shapes and sizes. His was Buddy. He learned how to be a parent. He looked up at his dad and realized how much must go on to be an adult. They drive by the street where his house was heading in the direction of the mall where he asked his dad what they were doing.

"You'll see son."

They get out of the car and walk in and to his surprise a pet store. Confused but before he could ask his dad says, "Lance , your mom and I decided we watched how you took care of Buddy and taught him and yourself how to take care of each other. So we decided to get rid of Buddy was good for Buddy but not for you so if you want if can pick a puppy to replace Buddy."

"Dad, nothing can replace Buddy he was a fox BUT I can still get a puppy though." Lance laughed and had the biggest smile a ten year old could have. His dad laughed with him. They were in the pet store five minutes when one of the puppies got away from the employee and ran up to Lance. He scratched Lance's leg for attention and at that, the decision was made.

"This one dad!"

It was an English bulldog and his dad like him also. They bought the dog and named him Spike, like in Tom and Jerry.

Good old Spike lived ten years and Lance treated him like his own kin. Spike always made Lance happy and never did him wrong. Once someone hit the dog as they were walking past the backyard and Spike was barking at them. The kid threw a stick and hit the dog to make it yelp. Lance ran outside and saw the person. After tending to the dog making sure he was ok he ran after the kid. When he found the right time to confront the kid he took it. When the kid walked back through the park alone, Lance came up from behind and beat the kid up. The kid never saw it coming and Lance made he extracted his avenge on the boy.

Maybe it was there the vigilante attitude or the judge like punishment was started. A genesis maybe in a sense. He knows his dad always was for the morally correct decisions but seemed unhappy. The morally correct weren't always as happy as the incorrect His dad was a good man but somewhat a pacifist. A happy go lucky that seemed when confronted with a situation with someone he would back down and not come out of it with his point made or maybe being benefited from the situation. His dad in a way was too nice. That is where they are different. Lance doesn't back down his point will be made definitively or subtlety. He knows there are times he was wrong but facts can be wrong not opinions. You can't have an opinion and be told that was wrong. An opinion is what you think and no one can tell you what you think is wrong unless it was statement. Always wanting to stick up for the wronged person, or animal, Lance somehow always got his point across. Not always physical though.

Is a very smart guy but pays attention to his surroundings. He understands people, their thoughts and actions. He never passes up a chance to learn something new. This is what has led him to being an unknown figure in the murders. Always watching the victims knowing when to strike when it is best for both. He sees the light in the foreground and starts thinking about his plan of attack. He stoops and crawls up behind a bush. He sees no lights inside the house. The houses are about thirty five feet apart or so. The neighbor's lights are out and since they are somewhat distant from each other he doesn't feel they are a threat. He approaches closer to the house and sees no activity of any sort going on inside the home.

He thinks to himself, ok great he is not here so plan b looks like it is going to be. . He gives up on the notion that Cleters is not home till he gets inside. He decides to go to try the rear door for entrance. It is dark out back because oak trees back there are refusing to let the moonlight through. How perfect is this he thinks. Almost like God is cooperating and helping him go stealth. He tugs on the screen slider and gets to the interior door and to his surprise it is open. You got to be kidding me he thinks to himself, way too easy. Maybe he'll find Cleters gift wrapped with a big bow ready to go. He laughs to himself.

He looks inside and the house looks relatively clean and organized but still no sign of anyone. He hears nothing and decides to go in. He enters the back which is the kitchen and sees some boxes opened scattered throughout the kitchen and dining room. He proceeds carefully through the house to the stairway .The first floor is carpeted and being a newer house he moves around sound free. He looks around and assumes that Cleters is either a bachelor or divorced. There are no pictures outside of him and maybe his parents. No kids or females. That was one factor he was worried about having to deal with other family members. Lance decided he would wait till Cleters would come out of his house or when the other members left. Hoping that would that is. If not this was this was the only way the plan would be postponed.

He heads up the stairs quietly trying to keep his feet on the edges of the steps where they rarely crack since they are not used by normal foot traffic. The house has a lilac smell to it probably a plugged in fresheners in the house. He reaches the top where he looks left and sees two doors then to the right where he sees three doors but none have lights on in them. He looks down the steps and listens to make sure no one is coming in. He decides to head right and peeks into what looks like an office. The desk is littered with papers and the filing cabinet is left opened. Weird looks like he was robbed. He heads to the next room which when he opens the door is the bathroom. He turns around and proceeds to the other end of the hallway which has three doors and when he gets to the first door it is another spare room which has a bed and couple pieces of furniture but otherwise bare. The next room is like a den where he sees an Xbox and stereo system along with a stationary bike. He heads to the door at the end of the hall and opens it.

Well this it he thinks if he is not in he then he just is not there. He walks quietly to it not to disturb the silence that has filled the air. He looks in, the bed is made and no one is there.

Damn it. Lance wanted to make the prick suffer but now he knows he has to go the alternate route. He takes a look around and sees pictures of Cleters with other guys. Some are cops; others are at functions which are shirt and tie. Couple of him are in tuxedos. Looks like a dick thinks Lance.

Breathing out a sigh of disappointment he heads back out of the room and takes one final scan for maybe a set of keys for a car. He hasn't looked outside yet but now prays there is a vehicle out there. Since the guy lives alone ands is not home there maybe no car. He approaches the front window and peeks out making sure not to touch it to cause movement. He looks up and down the street and sees no cars. SHIT! He thinks to himself wait a minute wasn't this going so smooth at first and now shit is falling apart? Not trying to get too perturbed he sees no keys and heads down the stairs.

He goes from the front of the house to the kitchen and down a hall to the garage. He puts his hand on the knob and right before he opens it he closes his eyes and makes a quick wish that something is in there that he can use. He opens it almost reluctantly and there it is a car. The 2005 BMW candy apple red 4 door. Lance breathes a sigh of relief, well tonight is not a total waste he thinks. Now the next step finds the keys to the car. He heads back in through the hall, he goes to the kitchen and looks for where the keys maybe. He heads to the phone where a notepad is but doesn't see them. He uses his penlight, searches through the darkness and sees keys hanging on the wall. Ahh there we are. He goes to the three hooks where two are occupied with keys. He notices they are labeled and reads them. One says "shed" and the other says "sis". Are you fucking kidding me he thinks? He turns around and scours the counters –nothing. He opens a couple of drawers hoping to find them in there. He finds the utility drawer with a bunch of junk but no keys.

Starting to get worried he heads into the dining room where a desk is in the corner. He proceeds towards it and looks on the top. Damn there's a lot of crap here. This is making it tougher to get in and out having to hunt down the keys. Nothing again. He goes in the top drawer, sifting through the papers he comes up empty. He looks at his watch it is getting late. He doesn't want to get back to the lot where his car is the only car there and stands out. He knows he needs to pick up the pace considering now he has to drive to the warehouse with the BMW then walk back to the parking lot is tacking a considerable amount of time to his night. He can feel a tad bit of excitement start to overtake him. He takes a deep breath and calms himself down. This is nothing he hasn't done before so chill out he thinks to himself. He cuts through the darkness with his light and sees by the front door a little table with miscellaneous stuff on it. He pushes to the side some video membership cards and a gym card, and there they are, the BMW logo'd keys.

"Thank you" he says out loud knowing no one can hear him. Now it is time to plant the evidence he heads towards the door he came in and grabs his bag. He opens it up, reaches inside and pulls out a piece of metal that is small. It is unique enough that it can only come from the Hatsin warehouse. It is a piece that anyone in town would know where it came from. Now is where to leave it in an inconspicuous spot that stands out and yet doesn't stand out. He decides to leave it outside lying in the mulch by the door he had entered through. He closes the door and walks through the kitchen to the garage door. He looks around and is somewhat confused where he stands now that no one was there. Oh well, he thinks. At least the plan can still get accomplished.

He opens the garage door and looks down at his hands. He checks to make sure everything he came with is leaving with him. He heads towards one of the windows and looks out to see if anyone is outside. The houses are all dark and the streets are as naked as could be. He plans which direction he will pull out and head. He turns back around and opens the door to the car. He throws the bag in the car and jumps in he at first has to get his bearings right on the car and looks for the ignition and once he finds it, he starts the car. He looks up, sees the garage opener and presses the button. The door slowly opens the door and it opens quietly which doesn't hurt the situation. He pulls out slowly and when he clears the door he hits the garage opener to close the door. He puts the car in the forward and heads down the street.

He drives towards the warehouse making sure to make no errors and get caught he is not far off and is planning if he should make sure Smythe is still with the plan. He sees the warehouse a few blocks away and reaches for his gym bag making sure it is ready to go. He turns his lights out and uses the moonlight as his flashlight pulling into the rear of the building. Once he pulls up to the ramp which does blend with all the scrap iron and trash laying around he turns on his parking lights for guidance. He goes down the ramp till he gets to the door where he gets out and goes through a man door to the side where he turns on his flashlight to get to the garage door to open it. He slowly raises the battered screechy door. He pulls the door towards himself to prevent the door from scraping the metal track. Once it is high enough he goes back to the car, jumps in and pulls it into the warehouse being carefully not to knock anything over to make noise. He puts in park and gets out heading back to the overhead door to close it. Once closed he turns on his flashlight and grabs the gym bag and opens it. He pulls out a gun then proceeds to the rear of the car where he pops the trunk and places the gun in it .From there he goes back to the bag, grabs the throw away cell phone and places it top of the car.

He grabs the bag and checks the area over for anything he may have left. After being satisfied he heads out of the room and goes through a couple of doors where he goes to a table and places a paper bag on it. He uses his flashlight to get out of the warehouse.

He reaches a door which leads out of the building where he leaves. Being sure he turns out his light and takes his time leaving the property. There are no cars or sounds around the area. It is quiet, too quiet. His heart is racing where he can feel it beating through his shirt. Almost with a pulse that and pounding that he thinks his shirt is moving to. He hasn't had an adrenaline rush like this since his last murder. " Ahh soon this will be all over." He thinks to himself. He picks up the pace and tries to scurry out of the area. He has about 10 more minutes walking. He doesn't want to run and draw attention to himself. He tries to move amongst the shadows so not to be noticed. He checks his clock and it is almost 10 pm. He figures he should be back home by 1030 at the latest and maybe catch a rerun of CSI. He will go to bed then go to work tomorrow and after that he will find John and set up the rest of the plan .He feels a little uncomfortable leaving the car by itself with all the other stuff laying for someone to find. His luck some homeless guy will ruin it all and it is back to the drawing board for him. For months he has terrorized the area and now the Wishbone Killer will be put to rest.

He comes up on an intersection and sees the mall lot across the street. He heads through the brush to get to the area where his car is parked. Before he enters the lighted area he scours the area for any people. After waiting few seconds he feels the coast is clear and advances to his car. He opens his door and throws in the bag. He starts the car and looks in the rear view but before pulling out he smiles to himself and says" You are almost there, Lance, almost there." With that he pulls out and heads home. It is about for the nightly bowl of ice cream anyways he realizes.

The next day Lance gets up early. Today is the day. He barely slept his mind kept running through the agenda. It was either thoughts of getting caught or living his life like he has finally planned have been getting toggled throughout the night.

He picks up the phone then calls his work and uses a sick day. Since he calls out so infrequently there are no questions asked of him. He will tell Jill he didn't feel well during the night and wanted to be safe and called out. He then reaches towards the alarm clock. He turns the alarm off before it gets to the set time. He heads into the bathroom performs his ritual and gets dressed. He goes downstairs and greets Jill who comes into the front door. "Hi honey. How was work?" he gives her a kiss on the cheek as she gives him a hug.

"You know long night but I like my job. Anything happen while I was gone? Why are you dressed like that? No work today?" she asks inquisitively.

"I didn't feel good through the night then figured I would use a sick day and be safe. Outside of that my night wasn't too bad. Nothing happened just went to bed after watching Tombstone."

"For what the two hundredth time?" she says with a snicker.

"Oh you are so funny. After that had some ice cream and then went to bed."

He gets out the cereal and has a small bowl. He forces himself to eat what little he has poured. He has no appetite. He offers Jill to make her breakfast but she is satisfied with just a bowl of cereal.

"Do you need anything while I am out?" he asks her.

"Well I think I am good. Don't spend much wait till the weekend when we grocery shop. What are you getting though?"

Hurry, think quick Lance of all the stuff you have planned you didn't have answer for what you were going to the store for. "Umm. Some cold medicine and maybe some TUMS."

"Oh ok. Well pick me up some deodorant."

"Ok no problem. I will be back." He moves slowly around the house trying to act like he is somewhat under the weather.

"Why do you seem happy if you don't feel good?"She asks him.

"Because I am just happy. For some reason I woke up realizing there is nothing in this world I want more then to be with you. I think this weekend I am taking you away for a surprise."

"Oh really? Wow what has brought this on?" she asks him smiling and coming up to him and starts to hug him.

"Nothing .Just you are very special to me and I want to show you and sometimes I lose track of the important little things."He hugs her back. With the hug he feels the relief subduing him from eliminating the evil that controls his life.

"Ok hey I am not going to complain that you are going to spoil me."

"Good don't"he says smiling.

He gives her a quick kiss then grabs his jacket and heads out. He plans on going to Wal-mart and heading to see John pestering the customers out front. He uses some money he had saved in his drawer to give to John as an incentive to get him to the warehouse later in the day. Afterwards he plans on coming home immediately afterwards and doing house work till about 220 or so and then head back to Wal-mart and see if John took him up on his offer. If John doesn't, he plans on coaxing John into his vehicle and somewhat altering the plan to an extent. He just hopes it doesn't go that far.

He gets in his vehicle and pulls out. He sees Jill at the front window and waves to her. She heads away from the window and Lance heads to Wal-mart. Within a few minutes he is there. He pulls into the lot and finds a spot not too far from the store. He gets out of the car and scans the front of the store looking for John. He doesn't see him out front and slows the pace down trying to find him. He then notices John down off to the west and starts walking in that direction where he gets within fifty feet and no one is around them. John sees him coming, pauses and then starts to yell at Lance. "You here to give me some money if not then get the hell away from me if you know what is good for you."

Lance bites his tongue he knows he needs to play this cool.

"Actually John I am here to give you money. I have a proposition for you. You can make money for the next few weeks and it is not that tough of a job."

John looks at him puzzled not expecting Lance to be kind, let alone give him money after what their past has brought them. "Really" he says. "kidding me? After I almost kicked your ass you now want to be my friend?"

"No I don't want to be your friend. I figured I would be nice and help you out. You could say it is my good deed of the day."

"I don't take God damn hand outs. I choose to be like this. I choose to make my statement by living this way."

"How is that? Living off of trash and having nowhere to call home?" asks Lance getting annoyed at the foolishness coming from the bum's mouth. He must be careful though and not to scare him off and shooting himself in the foot.

"I am living off of the people like you. I have no job, no place to call home. I have no bills and I have no friends to pester me for money or do them favors that I will never get in return. It is the people who have all that I don't that keep me living. I live off of them and don't have the stress or guilt of having to perform to other's expectations. "He points towards the people walking into Wal-mart. These are the people he is referring to. He looks at Lance and keeps his eye contact with him through out his lecture where Lance does not succumb to the stare nor the conversation.

"So tell me Mr. College educated guy why would I want to do anything for me if I am not unhappy?"

Lance pauses and realizes he needs to come up with a new angle. The original angle now seems moot. Think fast Lance. We can't lose this guy. What can coach him into agreeing with Lance into helping. He comes up with an answer.

"Listen John. I am not trying to insult you. I know you had a tough time recently with falsely being accused of the kidnapping a possible rape of the little girl and maybe if you show you have a part time job doing something maybe it will help out your image or ,hell maybe you would need the money for a lawyer if that is what you needed." Lance takes a deep breath and is actually proud of himself. Not too shabby makes sense. Only problem was not blowing a gasket about the little girl and needing to pretend. He thinks Smythe is innocent and the whole incident is a mistake. Damn that hurt but revenge will be sweet. It is only a little time away. Smythe looks at him and looks like he is pondering what to do. After a minute Smythe answers him.

"Well I didn't do anything to any little girl" He says it but stutters all over himself while not once making eye contact with Lance. "Since people are so quick to judge I guess maybe this can help me out in either circumstance."

"So do we have a deal then"? You have nothing to lose. About four to six hours a day about four to five days a week. I will be paying you cash and lunch is on me." Lance has made the offer sound very lucrative but will Smythe take it?

After Smythe walks round looking at the ground for loose change he heads back towards Lance and asks him a question. Lance is unsure what is about to come out of his mouth and hopes he doesn't need to resort to taking an alternative route which most likely alter everything he planned. "What do I need to do? How much are we talking?" The look is Smythe's eye is that of hope and Lance can see he pretty much has him latched and now for the close.

"There is a warehouse about five minutes from here. You can meet me there and I have supplies there for you. You will be cleaning up trash and organizing the place because I am moving my business into there within a couple of weeks. I plan..."
Before he can finish his sentence Lance is interrupted.
"Listen I don't have to move heavy stuff does me? I have a bad back but I think I can still do the job."
"Don't worry about it. I will make sure nothing heavy will be needed to be moved. The pay is $10 an hour under the table. Sound good?"
Before Lance can take another breath Smythe answers him and agrees to the deal.
"I will do it. Where is this warehouse?"
"Familiar with the Hatsin Building?"
First looking puzzled Smythe answers." Yes I do, not real good though."
"That is fine. Go around the rear of the building and you walk down a driveway which at the bottom has an overhead door and then you will see a blue man door to the right of it. Go through that door then head through that room to the room to the left being sure to close the door behind you. There are plenty cats around there and they try sneaking into the warehouse through that door. I will meet you there around say 330 pm today?"
"That sounds good. Am I working all night?"
"NO just a couple of hours then the next day we start early. Just wear whatever you want. Any other questions?"
"No I guess I am good. I am only doing this because of my misperceived reputation."
"Oh I understand. Everyone gets their due." Lance knows he shortly will put an end to the lies of this sick pervert.
"Well I will see you later. By the way don't let anyone else know. I only have enough money for one person and you are the person I chose."
"Not sure why but thanks." Smythe says.
"Do you have a watch?"

"NO but the bank clock is never wrong and that is what I go buy." He points to the bank clock across the lot.

"Ok remember 330.OK?"

"Yes."

With that Lance walks away and heads towards his car. He walks back there and feels good. So far so good. Everything he was worried about is falling into spot.

About twenty five feet from his vehicle he realizes he has to go into the store and pick up some stuff. He reroutes himself and heads into the store. He has everything set up at the warehouse so all he needs to do there is get there early enough to activate the plan. He walks around the store and picks up the stuff he told Jill he was getting He turns down the pet food aisle and hears his name getting called out.

"Hey Lance."

He turns around and sees from the Giant.

"Hey how are you?"

"I am good. I just came to get a toaster. Mine broke this morning and I can't eat a bagel without toasting it."

"Oh I agree."

They move to the side so they do not block the aisle.

"So this is the little guy? He is so cute. Looks like his mom. "Lance leans over looking at the baby. He touches the baby's hand.

"Thank you. If you like him so much you can take him home and get up with him through the night. I'll even pay for the formula."

Lance looks at her and is so happy he has befriended her. She is the prototype of the person he believes he defends almost like a super hero.

"How about I take a rain check on that? He is so quiet. IS he typically like this?"

"Pretty much he is quiet except at night. He has his days and nights mixed up though. "

"Ah give it time." He looks in her cart and notices and the baby stuff she has bought. He notices nothing for anyone else, he always had the perception she cared about no one except her child...

"So how is everything?" he asks her.

"Pretty good just have the day off and have some errands I have to run. What brings you here?"

"Same as you I have a few things to pick up. My girlfriend has sent me for a few items."

"Oh really? She making you breakfast in return?" Amy asks with a heart laugh.

"And lunch too." replies Lance back to her. Matching her hearty laugh.

"What a good woman. By the way guess what?"

"What?"

"Sky High has flown the coupe. No one can find him and some people believe he has left the area. Maybe some dealers came after him and killed him. Regardless it has been peaceful at work and in my neighborhood since he has been gone."

"Are you serious he is missing? Did they call the police?"

"Hell no police probably would have a party .They could care less if a dealer is missing. Just means kids are a little safer with one less as in the town."

Exactly Lance thinks to himself .The police have bigger issues such as a serial murderer and they probably are praying Sky was a victim to him anyway. No chance they are going to spend a minute on a missing big time drug dealer.

"If we are lucky he is at the bottom of the sewer with some rats." Lance states.

"We couldn't be lucky enough." She says with a laugh.

Lance laughs with her and thinks if you only knew.

"Well I better pick up the pace my food is probably getting cold. Take care and see you at the Giant."

"Ok Lance. See you soon." She turns around and walks away. Lance continues is shopping and thinks how she seemed relieved at the thought Sky was out of her life. Now that is what Lance does what he does for. People feeling happier and eliminating people who just deserve to be eliminated. Makes him feel better too and seeing she should be worried about taking care of her little and focusing on such an ass. He was a cute little kid too. For a moment Lance ponders what his child will look like .He is excited to be taking his child out and watching him grow. He smiles knowing it is just about time to start that life he craves.

He finishes getting what he needs and heads outside looking towards the direction Smythe was in but doesn't see him. He says a quick prayer and hopes he sees him later. He gets into his car and pulls out taking one more glance down the block still no Smythe. He will be there he convinces himself .He sure hopes so he is not in the mood for hunting today.

It is 337 pm at the Hatsin Warehouse. John Smythe walks through the eastern entrance door. He looks at the paper given to him and follows it to a room that has a BMW in it with a cell phone on top of the hood.

The phone rings and he walks towards it suspiciously and answers it.

"Hello?"

"Hey John, Ready to die."

"Wait a minute .What are you talking about? Who is this? Where are you?" asks Smythe confused at what is going on. He hears nothing but a low laugh. He recognizes that is it is Lance.

"What are you doing? I thought you needed help."

"No John it is time to pay the piper. "   "What the hell are you talking about?" says the bum starting to get loud into the phone.

"You know what I am talking about, the little girl you abducted and tried to rape. Tell me John did they teach you that in the war?"

"Fuck you. You know nothing about the war. I was killing people while you were wetting your diaper you punk!"

"Yes true John but guess what? I was killing people while you were trying to get lucky with a little girl. "

John is confused he responds."A yuppie bitch like you couldn't kill a fly. Your type turns it nose up on people like me. You think because you went to college you are something special. When it came to war you guys cried at night while we..."

"Shut the fuck up!! I am not like that I am the person who is like them on the outside but on the inside is where I differ. I eliminate those people you refer to. I do what people like you want done but will not do it. I kill the CEOs who make 7 figures and instead of skipping their big bonuses they lay off the less fortunate to keep those bonuses coming in. I kill the drug dealers too, the other end of the spectrum. Dealers who bring down the high or keep the low incomed down by trapping them into their web of addiction. Them I have your type John. The sick fuck who people would compare me to. This is where it ends I am done and you will be my last kill. To society after today you will be known as the Wish bone Killer."

With that there is then silence. John stands there and then realizes he is wrong. "You are the killer!!!?!? You killed all those people like you." the bum's face looks terrified.

"Yes I am but the difference is they were killed because they forgot what respect and human compassion was .Then they all were put in a position of power and decided that made them better people."

"Well why me then? I am a homeless person wh…"

"Who kidnapped a girl and tried to rape her for that I have gone against my reasoning of killing and decided you need to be punished. What you did was unacceptable and life has no room for sickos like you" Lance also thinks to himself that also being the way out of this and pinning it on the bum was another reason.

"Just like that girl you tried to rape you will know what fear is."

"You bastard fuck. Show yourself so I can kick your ass! I have beaten coward fucks like you in the war."

"SHUT UP!! I hold the cards here .You are a sick man .Thank God she got away. I believe you also have something to do with that woman. I can't let other innocent children or woman die because of you."

"Fuck you punk. Show yourself."

"You listen to me. If you listen maybe we can settle face to face. Go the car in front of you .The trunk is unlocked, open it and grab the gun."

"You crazy? Giving me a gun? "The bum hesitates to do it but makes his way to the car. He opens up the trunk and sees a shotgun in the trunk and grabs it. He is confused and asks." You must be kidding me." There is no reply .He looks at the phone .There is no longer a connection. He stands there and looks around. He is unsure what his next move is. He is quite baffled he tries to comprehend what is going on. He was under the foregone conclusion he was working for some money and now he seems to be in a twisted plot of his life and death.

Mason wakes up before the alarm clock goes off. He feels anxious this morning. He doesn't think he is sick but the slight rush he has is strange. He proceeds to go to work and the day goes relatively normal but today will be no normal day.

It is coming up on 325 pm at the police station where the agents and officers are discussing a possible new strategy.

Mason is at his desk getting ready for the briefing. He still can't put his finger on it but something is different. He feels like an answer is smacking him right in the face and yet he comes up with nothing.

"Ok, maybe we should come up with a new plan in case the killer kills the victim or gets another."Mitchell suggests to the group. He face looks worn. He is missing a lot of sleep .The past couple of days have been very productive and feels that the killer is nervous.

"Don't you think he is going to kill her?"

"No I hope he doesn't but something is different .He messed up here .The victim was on the phone and someone actually heard something. He has been to perfect to this victim. Why did he not kill this one at her place? Why chance someone coming out there and catching him? Something is not right."

Mason interjects. "Maybe he kidnapped and is going to use her for ransom? Or maybe try to find out what we know about him."

"Possibly but I doubt he will call us .I think he would want to give us no more clues then what he thinks we already have. There could be a chance she comes out of this alive. Try to link why this woman was picked out. If he messed on the timing maybe he messed up in other ways."

"Good idea, Mitch. I will call the lab and see if they came up anything yet." Tom states. The group gets up and heads towards the board hoping someone will come up with an angle that could be the big break. Just then a police dispatcher breaks into the room startling a few of the officers.

"Jesus, Mick. What the hell is…" before the captain can finish the dispatcher's face looks like it seen a ghost.

"Captain! There is a guy on the phone saying he saw a woman looking like Vicky being drug into the Hatsin old warehouse building about five minutes ago. She was screaming and he struck her."

"Is he still on the phone?"

"No he said he was going back to see if he could find more information out."

With that news the whole room buzzes. Men start running towards their chairs grabbing their jackets.

Mitchell races to the front of the room.

"Ok guys .This could be the break we have been waiting for. I want all units, agents and surrounding jurisdictions available and meet their in ten minutes. Mason and I will give info out over the radio on where to set up for all units. I want this place surrounded before anyone makes a move into the place we may only get one shot and this is it." Almost screaming the instructions the room has filled with every living body in the station. The men can tell the urgency in his voice the adrenaline is rushing through his and everyone else's veins.

"Our goal is to find Victoria Ganes. If we do not find her we must NOT let the killer escape. Only shoot if shot upon. Account for everyone in your units when going in. Enough people have been killed. The last thing anyone wants is to lose of one of us."

"Excuse me. What if we find her and the killer is evading us?"

Mason steps up to the podium and answers the question.

"Shoot him. If he is trying to escape and she is found I say shoot him to slow him down."

"Shoot to kill the bastard if that doesn't work" Is shouted from the rear of the room unknown of the source.

"Listen we know our jobs. We also known this is a sensitive issue for eight local people have been murdered and some of us knew them. I will leave it at this .Find her then whatever happens, happens."

Tom approaches the podium.

"We leave in 5 minutes. I want vests on guns loaded. Mitch, Mason and I will ride together .SWAT and the FBI are there way and told to wait a couple blocks of away but monitor the in and out of traffic. When we arrive we will give the signals. If he or she is found alert all others of the whereabouts and teams converge on the area but make sure someone is covering where you leave to be safe."

"Who is in charge on this raid sir? FBI or Local?"

Tom answers. "FBI but if we do not respond then Mason has all the power to decide what he feels."

Mitch steps back up to the podium." It is time for us to hustle. May God be with us all. Men let's find us a killer!"

With that the room empties .Captain Ron stays behind and handles the media telling them to report nothing or go nowhere till the word is given it is ok.

The agents and Mason jump in their Tahoe and head towards the warehouse. As they drive thoughts race through Mason's head. Finally this will be coming to an end. Many a night he lost sleep and tried to keep his sanity and now he may meet his nightmare face to face possibly. What will he do? Thoughts of hate go through his mind where he wants to just torture the bastard and at the same his conscious tells him to almost do the same thing.

The phone rings again and John answers it.

"You left me a gun with no bullets? You are a coward! Hide behind the phone and."

"Shut up! Now listen to me. There are no bullets in the gun. Follow the door to the left and it will lead to the bullets. Do you think I am just going to hand you everything? I want to have fun killing you."

At that moment Lance hangs up on John. Dumbfounded he looks around frantically. The bum heads out the door to a room with a shotgun shell on the floor. He heads back into the room getting into the car and looking for the keys He gets out of the car .He heads out of the room .where he enters. and when the door shuts it locks him out. He follows a series of doors that are open .It is very dark and cold. He walks up to a table and opens a bag. At that moment the phone rings.

"You bastard where are the bullets?

"Bullets?" Lance starts laughing." I must have forgotten to pack them. At least I gave you one so make the most of your chance. Now you no what feeling helpless is just like that little girl. "

The bum throws the bag with a shirt hanging out of it. "I want to see you!!! You fuckin coward stop hiding!!!"

"Quiet!!" screams Lance into the phone. Do you hear that? The cops are almost here and you have your chance to kill me or escape. Instead I will do this for you I will hunt you down and kill you, you worthless piece of shit. "

The bum starts looking around in a craze trying to find a way either out or just to find Lance.

"You asshole you are trying to set me up!!!" Looks around trying to find an exit. At the same time his head is convoluted with ideas of either trying to kill Lance or escape. He hears the sirens close to where he is at.

Mason tries to maintain his euphoric rush and show he is under control in front of the agents. He can feel his leg bouncing and hand fidgeting around the side door. It seems to take energy to maintain control. They are almost there and talk on where to place the teams. They meet up with the SWAT and other squads. They are about 2 blocks away. They get out of their car and approach the captain of the SWAT team.

"Bill Bast Had of the SWAT team."

"I am agent Mitchell Rakers and this is agent Tom. This is." Before he can proceed Bill interrupts.

"I know Mason. Hopefully this is it, Mace." He looks towards Mason and Mitchell catches the look in their eyes. He sees hope .A first time he has been around these men and feels they are ahead of the killer. In the back of his mind he hopes this ends it for the sake of the public and maybe most of all for the sake of the force whom is weary and morale is broken.

What do you have here Bill? I want us set up and ready to go in five minutes. I do not want this bastard to get away."

"Understandable. We have six entrances. I have four SWAT teams from surrounding areas almost doubled up around the perimeter. I have FBI agents with locals on the west and east. Over here I have locals, state and sheriff's men everywhere else. I am guessing we have a total of 120 men or so. I also have men around a 2 block area for safety in case he slips past us. Honestly agent we are well prepared."

Mitchell looks over the map he sees no problems but asks. "Any aerial?"

"Yes it is on its way and should be here when we go in." Bill adjusts his holster and looks anxious.

"Any questions?" Bill looks around.

Mitch responds." Mason and I will take this squad and Tom will take the west squad." Mitchell points at the map. They know the moment is near. They look at each other like a team in a huddle.

"Ok let's go. In three minutes I will check in with the squads when they are in position I will give the go and then we charge in."

Mason and Mitchell head towards the vehicle. They jump .Mitchell drives quickly towards their destination. They arrive in two minutes and see the building there is a silence while they get their gear on. The squad comes over to prepare for the raid

"I am Agent Mitchell and this is Mason. We will lead and any questions direct them at either of us."

"No problem sir. Let's just get this bastard."

"The group of five run towards the three story building and hide behind a broken down delivery truck. Mitchell gives the signal to halt. Mason can feel his leg shaking .The anticipation is driving him insane. He wants to hear that signal. The seconds go by but feel like minutes. It is so quiet for so much action going on. He can see the other squads getting in position. Then...

"Mitchell?" says a voice over the radio.

"We are ready" responds the agent.

"We will go in on three on my command." Says Bill. All units can hear him.

"One......Two....." The clock like stops it is an eternity. The squad all starts moving.

"Three!!!!!!!!!!"

Mitchell leads the squad towards the entrance with Mason following close behind. Both men are well armed. With a gun in their hand and one on the hip. The rest of the squad are carrying either hand guns or shotguns. The pace seems frantic. Everything that has happened has now come to this point. This is the climax. Mason's eyes are rapidly going from left to right like a cyclone in Battle star Galactica red eye.

Mason can hear commands and updates from the squads also raiding the building. The building is old and had been vacant for about 5 years. The rooms are big and cluttered with debris from the businesses that were there from before. It is cold, very cold. The building seems to almost deter heat.

"Mitch left or right?" Mason faces a hallway and asks for advice.

"We'll go left you take right. After you clear meet back here to go upstairs. Problems, yell!"

The squad splits into two. Mason and a SWAT member take to the rooms to the right to clear them and nothing is there. They can hear Mitch and team nearby.

"Clear here."

"Here too."

The team regroups and heads towards the stairs. Hey come to the top of the stairs and enter the area cautiously. Mason signals he will head to the right. Mitchell takes his men to the left.

"Mace there is nothing here. I see no forms of life. Are they sure this is the right site?"

"Yes .This place is very large with three floors. I believe there is a base."

"Agent Rakers." Calls out another voice.

"Yes?"

"This is Charlie squad .Where are you?"

"We are on the second floor about twenty feet away. Why is that?"

"We entered to the door east of you and we are on the first floor but we hear noises from below."

"Did you check the other squads?"

"Sure did. Not them."

The excitement is Mitchell's voice is apparent. He looks at Mason and they signal to there squad to head back down.

"Hold your position .I am coming back down. Mason where was the basemen stairs? I didn't see them."

"Nor did I. Bill you there?"

"Go head Mace."

"Shoot me a copy of the blueprints. We want to go downstairs to the basement."

"No problem .You have your PDA?"

"Yep."

"k."

Mason gets a copy of the prints. He reviews them. The team gathers around the base of the stairs.

"Hey Mitch I can't find the stairway. "

Mitchell looks at PDA but as he is about to answer.

"Agent Rakers I suggest you hurry the sounds are moving."

"We can't find a stairway!"

"What is the revision of the prints?"

"1960."

"That is why the stairway was closed off before that and there are bilco doors probably buried under the trash."

"So how the fuck do we get down there?"

"Go through the kitchen to a door near the window. It is a closet but there is another door behind some shelves."

"Gotcha ya. I'll get back to you. Let's go men. "

They head towards the kitchen they run through the rooms knowing the exits are covered and the area had been cleared.

"There it is!!" Points out one of the men.

The frantic pace looking for a door continues .There are three. One of the men find it.

"Here it is!!"

The group comes to the door and looks for another door.

"What the fuck is that??!"

They listen they hear a door slamming and footsteps running down below.

"It's him. Find the Goddamn knob!!!"

Junk starts getting thrown out of the closet which is about 8 foot by 6 foot loaded with lots if shelving and junk.

"Found it!!!"

Mason yanks on the knob pushing the junk behind the door. They look down the steps and Mitchell starts leading them down where a dim light is visible. The smell is musky and gets colder by the step.

"We are downstairs and heading east. All teams hold you positions do not move unless told!!"

"Hey Mitch there is a light over here. "They head towards the light. As the approach he door they can hear footsteps not far away on the other side.

"Move!!!It's him!!!"

They break through the door and see a figure running down a hall and into a room to the left. They follow.

"Stop!!!" yells Mason but the man keeps running. The squad splits into two groups." Go that way it leads to the same spot." Directs Mitchell.

Mason takes one SWAT member and the head towards the other door. Both groups meet up in the room.

"Where did he go?" Their hearts are racing they are so close.

"There is one other way behind this door .Let's go then it splits up. We can't let him get to the split. Shit!! Hey Bill?!"

Go ahead!!"

"Anything up there?"

"We hear running below us but we are holding the exits."

"Ok all teams maintain positions. We are going into the south wing."

"Remember Agent Rakers those prints are not the original so there are rooms and halls not being reflected!"

"Thanks it is considered."

"Where to Mitch?"

Through this door we then split up and head east and west.

"Let's go"

The squad heads towards the door as they approach they hear footsteps running on the other side. They pause.

The steps are getting louder. The man is heading towards the door.

"Jesus he's coming out us!!!!" At that moment all the guns are raised and pointed at the door. Their bodies frozen with fear, anticipation and adrenaline. His finger dances on the trigger. They hear a scream getting louder from the other side of the door. Sweat starts dripping from his face and he wipes it quickly. Not knowing what is coming at them has made the situation scarier. The scream is chilling. Like from an injured animal but this is not an animal, who murders and mutilates for fun?

Mason thinks for a second this is a trap. As he is about to yell out the footsteps are outside the door and moving fast. Again time has almost stopped he looks at Mitchell who glances at him. They can read each others thoughts. This is it something will come to an end, only question is for whom.

Out the corner of his eye he catches the door starting to open he breaks his look from Mitchell.

"FBI stop!!!!!!"

"Here he comes!!!"

The door opens fully. The figure is in plain sight. Running at them with no hesitation they open fire .The figure at first doesn't seem to stop. He is lunging at Mason and is 10 feet away. Mason empties his clip into him. For a second he does think this guy can die then the body just stops and falls to his knees face down into the ground.

His gunfire has stopped. There is a mist of smoke from all the guns. It is so quiet Mason can hear the whole squad breathing. Everyone's eyes focused on the body on the ground. Mason approaches and kicks the body. Nothing. He reaches down and checks his pulse. Nothing.

"Agent Rakers!!???"

"We are fine .We have killed the killer. I repeat we have killed the killer!!" A cheer is heard from the distant. It is over.

Mason turns over the body.

"You know him?"

Mason looks over the body almost dazed.

"Yeah it is the crazy bum from Wal-mart. "

Mitchell approaches him"That is it!!"

"What?" replies Mason. "The link. This is how he did it. They went to Wal-mart and he tracked them from there."

"I guess." Says Mason sounding unsure.

"Agent Rakers? Can you come here?" calls a voice from another room.

Mitchell heads to the other room He walks in where the officer is standing. There is a body at the other end of the room in a chair. They walk towards it.

"Is it her?"

"No, it is a male. Actually the missing guy from a few weeks ago. He looks like his throat has been ripped out."

"Actually officer it has been burned out. You see the dried bubbles around the throat? That is a chemical burning the flesh and reacting to the skin."

They look around and see tools and objects laying and bloody." I guess this was the torture chamber."

Mitchell calls out." Ok all teams look for the girl."

He walks towards Mason. "We found the missing guy. It is ugly. We will look for the girl maybe you can address the media and clear them back some? Also great job. You are a good man. It has been a pleasure working with you." He puts his hand out to Mason and they shake, the stress seems to dissolve at the handshake.

"Sounds good. We find her and then it is all over. I appreciate your experience and have learned a lot from you. Thank you." Mason heads towards the stairs slowly. Happy but yet unsatisfied. He rethinks the last ten minutes of what just happened. His life flashed around him. Two months of nightmares are now over the people of the town can now sleep knowing they will be alive the next day. Mason heads out of the room and up the steps.

Meanwhile in a small house about ten miles away a television set is on with an interruption in the programming.

"We interrupt your program for this news breaking event in relation to the Wishbone Killer. According to sources the killer has been trapped inside a vacant warehouse on the eastern outskirts of the town for fifteen minutes. We are now going to the town of Ptown where Bill Shedar is live with this update. What can you tell us Bill? Do they indeed have the Wishbone Killer?"

"Thanks Mike. According to authorities at 215 today about twenty minutes ago, FBI and local authorities converged on a vacant warehouse on Miles St. Tips have held police to believe the killer was inside the warehouse .At that moment police had left the station and came here .They surrounded the building as you see behind me and then invaded the building at all first floor entrances to make sure there would be no uncovered ways out. Now since this invasion there had been yelling and then shots were fired. We are waiting to be told if the killer was found. "

"Ok Bill have there been any casualties?"

"No. Just shots"

"Have police said Victoria Ganes was here too?"

"Unfortunately her name has not been brought up. We hope that she is found safe."

"What is the feeling around there right now?"

"It is euphoric .There is about 60 officers and 30 FBI agents here buzzing around. When the word was told that the killer was here the mood picked up instantly to where it was like a team breaking from the huddle and running towards the line."

"How did police get the tip, Bill?"

"We are not sure but rumor has it that it was a phone call. I can see from here that more officers are running in but there are no shots being fired. "

If you are just joining us we are live in Ptown where the Wishbone Killer is sa..."

"Hey Mike. I have to interrupt you but I can see Mason Kade, lead detective heading out of the building towards us. Also it sounds like a roar or something coming from the officers near him. I believe that might actually be a cheer. Yes I think it is I see some smiles. Hold on he is approaching the media."

The volume on the television is turned up and a silhouette on the chair leans forward.

"Ok I need some silence .I do not have much information but more will be provided as it is attained. I will tell you what I know and then answer questions for about 3-4 minutes."

The captain pauses almost like trying to slow down his speech. A relief or burden that has been lifted off of someo0ne's shoulders can be seen on his face.

"We had trapped the Wishbone Killer . Upon trapping we engaged the killer in a gunfight. The killer was fatally wounded. So I say this clearly to the public of Ptown. The Wishbone killer is dead. I repeat –the Killer is dead. You can now sleep with the security that no one else is going to die at the hands of this monster."

Back in front of the television a voice says out loud." Very very good but now it is my turn. Unfortunately for you Mason Kade more will die."

"Excuse me was Victoria Ganes found?"

Mason pauses then takes away his smile realizing the story is not over for some.

"No she hasn't but we are in a rescue mission here. We have a base that was his and we are sure we will find her and hopefully she will be fine."

There is laughter at the television from the silhouette becoming louder and heartier. The hand reaches for a hunter's knife where the figure then stands up. Not far from the room a sound is heard. A whimpering sound becoming louder and more desperate. Accompanying the sound there is a metal clanking. As you head towards the sound a table with gore magazines, chains, and knives coated with blood and other tools of torture lay around. The figure heads towards the doorway where the sound is louder. Going past a table and chair there is a wall, green paint faded and chipping, with a chain fastened to the wall. The chain is bouncing around the wall towards the floor like a fish at the end of a line trying to escape. Instead of a fish though there is a person bloodied and scantly dressed. It is a battered woman. Her name is Victoria Ganes.

Her attempts screaming through the gag are moot .No one can hear them. Her eyes swollen with fear, the ground underneath her is wet from urinating; along with veins trying to break through the skin confirm she is aware death is near.

The figure approaches the tattered body. The approach almost seems like time has stopped. The figure stands above the woman. Her screams and tugs of the chain have stopped. She now knows her efforts are in vain and accepts what God has in store for her.

As the arm raises her eyes drop down away from the body and catches a glimpse of a vest on the chair. As the arm comes down and not being able to watch her killer, she fixes her eyes on a white label on the blue vest. She feels the top of her head get warm as the blood runs down her forehead. As the blood runs into her eyes and starts blurring her vision she focuses on a word on the vest. The word -Robert.